S0-ARO-319

EXT.

X - 4684

LARGE PRINT STR
Stroby, Wallace.
Gone 'til November

DISCARDED

EXTENSION DEPARTMENT
ROCHESTER PUBLIC LIBRARY
115 SOUTH AVENUE
ROCHESTER, NY 14604-1896

JUL 12 2010

# GONE 'TIL NOVEMBER

This Large Print Book carries the
Seal of Approval of N.A.V.H.

# GONE 'TIL NOVEMBER

## WALLACE STROBY

**THORNDIKE PRESS**

*A part of Gale, Cengage Learning*

Extension Department
Central Library of
Rochester and Monroe County
115 South Avenue
Rochester, New York 14604-1896

GALE
CENGAGE Learning

Detroit • New York • San Francisco • New Haven, Conn • Waterville, Maine • London

**GALE**
CENGAGE Learning™

Copyright © 2009 by Wallace Stroby.
Thorndike Press, a part of Gale, Cengage Learning.

**ALL RIGHTS RESERVED**
This is a work of fiction. All of the characters, organizations, and events portrayed in this novel are either products of the author's imagination or are used fictitiously.

Thorndike Press® Large Print Thriller.
The text of this Large Print edition is unabridged.
Other aspects of the book may vary from the original edition.
Set in 16 pt. Plantin.

**LIBRARY OF CONGRESS CATALOGING-IN-PUBLICATION DATA**

Stroby, Wallace.
   Gone 'til November / by Wallace Stroby.
     p. cm. — (Thorndike Press large print thriller)
   ISBN-13: 978-1-4104-2542-3 (alk. paper)
   ISBN-10: 1-4104-2542-8 (alk. paper)
   1. Policewomen—Fiction. 2. Murder—Investigation—Fiction.
3. Large type books. I. Title.
PS3619.T755G66 2010b
813'.6—dc22
                                     2009053622

Published in 2010 by arrangement with St. Martin's Press, LLC.

Printed in the United States of America
1 2 3 4 5 6 7 14 13 12 11 10

Extension Department
Central Library of
Rochester and Monroe County
115 South Avenue
Rochester, New York 14604-1896

*For Jack S. Smith and Jack D. Hunter*
*Flagler College 1981–82*

# ACKNOWLEDGMENTS

For reasons too numerous to mention, my thanks to friends new and old for their encouragement and support, especially Mark Voglesong, John Tinseth, James O. Born, Matt Seitz, and Brian and Donna Washburn. And, as always, to my mother, Inez Stroby, a single mom late in life who somehow made it all work. Much love and respect to all.

# ONE

Sara steered the cruiser onto the shoulder, saw what was ahead, thought, *Bad news.*

Gravel crunched under the tires as the Crown Vic settled at an angle. The radio crackled.

"Eight-seventeen, are you on scene?" Angie, the night dispatcher. "Have you responded?"

Sara lifted the dash mike, keyed it. "Eight-seventeen here. On scene now. Will advise."

In the blaze of her headlights, Billy stood behind his own green-and-white cruiser, looking off into the swamp, hands on his hips. Farther up on the shoulder was a gray late-model Honda Accord, trunk open. Blue, red, and yellow lights bathed the night.

She replaced the mike, tried to memorize the scene, wishing the grants had come through for the dashboard video cameras. She looked at her watch. Two ten.

Billy turned toward her, face blank. She

could see his jaws moving. He was chewing gum. After a moment, he looked back at the swamp.

She hadn't seen him at the Sheriff's Office, but she'd known he was on duty tonight, had heard him on the scanner. Part of her had hoped they'd cross paths before shift's end, part of her didn't. When she'd gotten the call, shots fired, she'd feared the worst. Now here he was, staring out into the swamp, looking lost.

*What have you done, Billy Boy? And why did you have to do it on my shift?*

She opened the door, took her portable radio from the passenger seat, and stepped out onto gravel. She fit the radio into its holder on her duty belt and plugged in the body mike clipped to her left shoulder. Her thumb slipped the holster loop that held the Glock in place on her right hip.

The air was thick, the heat oppressive after the air-conditioned cruiser. Hot for mid-October. No moon, but a sky full of stars.

The Honda had New Jersey plates. Billy had parked behind it, angled to the left, in the standard motor vehicle stop position, so the cruiser would protect him from oncoming traffic when he got out.

He half-turned. "Hey, Sara."

"Hey, Billy. You all right?"

He looked away from her, back at the swamp.

She had her hair tied up in back, could feel sweat form at the nape of her neck, drip beneath the Kevlar vest under her uniform shirt. She came up to stand beside him, followed his gaze. They were looking down a slight incline to the edge of the swamp. There was a patch of sodden grass, then a deeper dark where the trees started, Spanish moss hanging from them like cotton. In the grass, just short of the trees, a man lay facedown, right leg twisted under left, right arm extended.

"There he is," Billy said.

She looked around. She'd seen no traffic since she'd gotten the call, taken the turnoff for CR-23. Only locals used this route, few at night. To the east, acres and acres of sugarcane, then the distant glow of town. To the west, the gray ghosts of cypress trees, endless miles of wetlands stretching to Punta Gorda and the coast. She could smell the swamp, the rotten egg scent of sulfur.

The cruiser radios crackled in unison, the sound muffled by the closed doors. Off in the dark, as if in answer, bullfrogs sounded. Then another, deeper noise, the low bellowing of a gator. The light from their rollers painted the trees, the swamp, illuminated the body below.

"Is he dead?" she said.

He nodded. "Or close to it. He hasn't moved at all. EMTs on their way."

"I heard."

She took the heavy aluminum flashlight from the ring on her belt and pushed the button. The bright halogen beam leaped out into darkness. She swept it across the man's back. His head was turned to the right, and even from here she could see his eyes were open.

Chinos, blue dress shirt, a deep, dark stain between the shoulder blades, shirt soaked with blood. A black man, young, dressed too well to be from around here.

"I'm going to have a look," she said.

"Careful. You step into a chuckhole down there, you'll break your ankle."

She shifted the light to her left hand, took a step down the incline, her right hand resting on the Glock. She could hear sirens in the distance.

She picked her way down the slope. When she reached the grass, she felt it give spongily under her shoes, water coming up around them.

She shone the light along the wet ground, looking for snakes. Something moved and splashed in the darkness. The noise of the bullfrogs stopped for a moment, then started again.

The gun was about a foot from the man's right hand. She held the light on it. A blued revolver, .38 maybe, rubber grips. She made a grid with the flashlight beam, looking for another weapon, footprints. Nothing.

"Anyone else in the car?" she called up. The sirens closer now.

"No. Just him. I told him to stop. I told him."

She crouched, not letting her knees touch the ground. Up close, she could see the gold wire-rim glasses twisted beneath his face, one side still looped over his ear. He looked like a teenager, hair close-cropped, a small gold ring in his right earlobe. His eyes were wide.

She played the beam down the body. Left arm folded beneath, right outstretched as if pointing to the gun. The shoes were tan leather, polished, the upturned soles shiny and new. No way he could have run on this grass, gotten away.

She touched the side of his neck. A faint warmth, but no pulse.

From above her, Billy said, "He dead?"

"Yes. He's dead."

Something moved in the trees, and her hand fell to the Glock. A shadow separated itself from the blackness, took wing silently. She looked up, watched it fly away, etched for an instant against the stars, wondered what it was.

She went back up the incline, careful where she put her feet. When she reached the gravel, Billy was standing beside the Honda's open trunk.

"Check out this shit," he said.

She went over and shone the light inside. The trunk was empty except for a nylon gearbag, partially unzipped. She saw the glint of metal within.

"You look in there?" she said.

"Yeah. He was acting nervous, so I asked him to open the trunk. When I saw the bag inside, he took off. I told him to stop. When he got down there, he rounded on me, drew down."

His voice was unsteady. She looked at him, saw his eyes were wet.

Sirens rose and fell in the distance.

"Cold out here," he said. "When did it get so cold?"

He paused between words, chest rising and falling rapidly, as if he were hyperventilating. The onset of shock.

"You should sit in the car," she said. She tucked the flashlight under her arm, took the thin Kevlar gloves from her belt and pulled them on, punching the Vs of her fingers together to get the fit tight.

"I'm all right," he said.

"You don't look it."

She shone the flashlight into the bag, reached down and pulled the zippered edges apart. Inside was a boxy MAC-10 machine gun with a pistol grip and a dull black finish. Under it were two semiautomatic handguns: a chrome Smith and Wesson with rubber grips, a blue-steel Heckler and Koch, both 9 mm. Boxes of ammunition, extra magazines for the MAC-10. *No wonder he ran.*

She heard a noise, turned to see Billy bent over on the shoulder, hands on his knees. He spit his gum out, gagged, vomited thin and watery onto the gravel.

"I'm okay," he said. He raised a hand to ward her off. "I'm okay."

He spit, straightened, turned away from her, bent and waited, ready to vomit again. She could hear his rapid breathing. *He's going to pass out.*

He put his hands on his hips, sucking in air, getting his control back. She watched him for a moment, then walked around the Honda and shone the light through the windows. There was a folded Florida map on the front passenger floor. In back was a

child safety seat and a brown leather overnight bag.

"He has a kid," Billy said. "You see that
seat? He has a kid."

*Maybe not.*

She looked down the road. Coming over a
small crest, she could see emergency lights
— two cruisers and an EMT van.

She looked at him.

"Anything you want to tell me before the
sheriff gets here?" she said.

He looked at the approaching cruisers,
then back at her, shook his head.

"No," he said. "I'm sorry, Sara. I never
had a choice."

"You did what you had to do. It'll be all
right."

Sirens all around them, the cruisers pulling up abreast of her own, the EMT truck
pulling ahead. She moved closer to Billy,
stood beside him.

The sirens rose, fell, and died. Car doors
opened and closed around them. They
stood together in the nexus of rolling lights.

She looked up, saw the far-off silhouette
of a bird against the starfield. An instant
later, it was gone. She wondered if it was
ever there at all.

"Well," Sheriff Hammond said. "What's

your take on this mess?"

They were in his office, the door shut. Floor-to-ceiling windows looked out on the rest of the station. Through the window behind his desk, she could see the small stretch of lawn lined with whitewashed stone, a bare flagpole lit by flood-lamps.

Four A.M. and he was in jeans and flannel shirt, unshaven. His hair was longish, his nose laced with broken blood vessels. He was from Mississippi, had come east thirty years ago but never lost that soft accent.

Sara had a bottle of water from the break-room vending machine but hadn't touched it yet. She wished she had an aspirin. It was her first midnight shift in months, and she'd been tired all night. Now she could feel the familiar beginnings of a migraine, the pulsing of a vein in her temple.

"From what I saw," she said, "it looks like it played out the way he told it. I responded as soon as I got the call. There wasn't a whole lot of time between the stop and when I got there."

He took an unsharpened pencil off the desk and leaned back in his chair. His desktop was cluttered, a bundle of papers held down by a dummy hand grenade he'd brought home from Vietnam, wire IN and OUT baskets, a framed photo of his daughter

17

as a teenager.

On a credenza behind him was a computer, shut down for the night. Beside it, in a plastic liner, was his sheriff's campaign hat, which he wore only on formal occasions. When he'd taken over the Sheriff's Office, he'd discontinued the use of their Smokey the Bear hats, opted for black baseball caps instead, and then made those optional as well, a change Sara had always been grateful for.

He scratched his jaw, tapped the pencil on the edge of the desk. She could sense his awkwardness.

"The lawyer from the Fraternal Order of Police is on his way," he said. "Boone from the state attorney's office in La Belle is still at the scene, but he'll roll back here soon. He'll be talking with you as well. That might be a little uncomfortable."

"Why's that?"

"He'll have to know about you two."

*Doesn't everybody already?*

She cracked the cap on the bottle, drank, replaced it.

"I understand that, Sheriff. But just for the record, that was over two years ago."

"I know. I'm just saying. Small county like this, small town, small department. If we don't tell him, someone else will. It's better

18

it come from us."

"I'll tell him."

"You're a woman in an otherwise all-male department, Sara. That puts you in a unique position. It's not fair, and I know it, but sometimes you have to be realistic about what other people might be thinking."

"I understand."

"This your first overnight in what, eight months?"

"Nine."

"Your first shift with him that entire time?"

She nodded, sipped more water, set the bottle on the floor. He pulled a yellow legal pad across the desk toward him.

"They ID the driver yet?" she said. She was feeling 4:00 A.M. fatigue, a slight dislocation from everything around her. The adrenaline was fading, and she wanted sleep.

He tilted the pad to read it.

"Derek Willis," he said. "Twenty-two. Had a current driver's license on him. A resident of Newark, New Jersey, and only one arrest, a misdemeanor joyriding charge. Ran him through NCIS. No hits."

"That the name on the registration?"

"No. Car's registered to a Wendell Abernathy, also of Newark. No hits on him either."

"FDLE involved?"

"Not yet."

"Good," she said.

"That could change, based on what Boone finds. If he feels he needs to bring them in, he will."

"Whatever the situation, this Willis wasn't a tourist, out there in the middle of the night, weapons in the trunk."

"I expect not."

"And what was he doing on that road in the first place? There's nothing out there for miles. If you're just passing through, heading south, interstate's easier, safer."

"Hopefully, all questions which will be answered."

She drank more water, put the bottle down, rubbed her left temple.

"Who's watching the little guy?" he said.

"JoBeth. She's at my house."

"JoBeth Ryan?"

"She's driving now, so it's easier for her."

"JoBeth's a good kid. And her father's a good man. She babysit for you a lot?"

"She's good with Danny. He likes her."

"How's he doing?"

"He has good days, bad days. The chemo's been rough."

"You ever hear from his father?"

She shook her head, looked away.

"I'm sorry," he said. "It's none of my business."

"It's okay. There's just not much to say. We're getting on with our lives, you know? We have to."

"Don't we all."

"They find anything else in the car?"

"Not so far. Howie's got it at the garage. We'll take it apart tomorrow, see what we find. I'm sorry, Sara, I was out of line there."

"It's all right. What's the ME say?"

"Not much yet." He tapped the pencil on his knee, relieved the subject had changed. "Three rounds, all from Flynn's Glock. Two in the chest" — he touched himself there — "one on the left side. One exit wound through the back. Looks like they were definitely facing each other when the first shots were fired, which is good news. He spun as he went down, which is how he caught the third round. His weapon hadn't been fired. Loaded, though. We're trying to track down next of kin. I've got a call in to someone I know at the state police up there as well."

Outside the window, it was almost dawn.

"You should sign out, get some sleep," he said.

She picked up the bottle, stood, felt the stiffness in her knees. She looked out into

21

the station, saw Angie, the big-haired bottle-blond dispatcher, watching her. Sara met her eyes until she looked away.

"You're on Monday to Friday, right?" he said.

"Yes."

"Good. So you've got the weekend in front of you. Come Monday, you go back on regular day shift?"

She nodded.

"Then take another twenty-four if you need to. We can cover. Just call Laurel, let her know."

"I'll be okay."

"You can decide that Sunday night. Boone's going to be calling you tomorrow, and you'll need to come in for the interview."

"I know."

She pressed her lower back, stretched. Through an open door she could see Billy talking to Sam Elwood, their chief deputy and internal affairs officer. He sat in a chair alongside Elwood's desk, elbows on his knees, head in his hands, staring at the floor. The real interview would start when Boone and the FOP lawyer got there.

"He's coasting on adrenaline right now," Hammond said, "but when all this hits home, it'll hit hard. We'll keep him out for a while, with pay, until this gets sorted, then bring him back on the desk, ease him into it. I've seen what this can do to men. Some can handle it. Some can't."

She watched Billy run a hand through his hair. He looked like a little boy waiting to be punished, bent over in his chair. She felt a sudden surge of affection for him, wanted to go in there, touch him, tell him everything would be okay. But she couldn't, wouldn't.

When she left the office, she saw him look up, meeting her eyes from across the room. Elwood looked, too, saw her, turned back to Billy and spoke. Billy held eye contact with her for a moment, then turned to answer.

She went out past the dispatcher's desk. Angie nodded at her without speaking. Sara pushed through the big glass door and out into the new morning.

She pulled the Blazer into the driveway, parked alongside JoBeth's Escort, shut off the engine. The sun was up, birds singing, and every muscle in her body felt stiff and sore.

She got out, locked the car with the keypad, slung her tactical bag over her shoulder, and went up the slate walk to the house. Danny's Big Wheel was on the lawn

23

where he'd left it yesterday. She picked it up by a handlebar, the plastic wet with dew, and moved it alongside the steps so no one would trip on it.

JoBeth was asleep on the living room couch, a blanket over her. She lay on her right side, left arm dangling almost to the carpet, the TV remote inches away on the rug, a cell phone alongside it. A science textbook and spiral notebook were on the coffee table.

The house was cool, the central air thrumming softly. She left her tac bag in the living room and went down the hall to Danny's room, the door half open. He slept facing the wall, his NASCAR comforter wrapped around him, a green stuffed dinosaur in his arms. Winnie-the-Pooh wallpaper in here, but she would have to change that soon. He'd grown out of it. On one wall they'd pinned a star map of constellations, on another a science timeline with dinosaur drawings that seemed to march across the wall in single file.

He was six, small for his age, hair cropped close but uneven where it had fallen out. She leaned against the doorjamb, watched his steady breathing. She often found herself doing this at night, coming in as quietly as she could, watching him to make sure he was still breathing, still here.

*It's not fair, what you've had to go through. But buddy, sometimes I love you so much I feel like my heart's going to explode. And I'm not going to let anything take you away from me.*

After a while she went down the hall to her bedroom. She locked the Glock and extra magazine in the strongbox on the closet shelf, pulled the hunter green uniform shirt off, and undid the Velcro snaps of the vest. The white T-shirt she wore beneath was soaked with sweat. She dropped the vest on the floor, the T-shirt atop it. She got the rest of her clothes off, left them where they lay.

In the bathroom, she undid her hair and ran the shower until it was hot. She climbed in and let the needles pound her neck and back where the muscles were stiffest, feeling some of the tension slip away. When she was done, she toweled off and put on sweatpants and a T-shirt, her hair still loose and wet. She took two Aleve, washed them down with a glass of water from the sink.

In the kitchen, she got two twenties from the flour canister. She found an envelope, put the bills inside, and wrote on the front of it: *JoBeth, short shift tonight, but I may need to go out for a while later today. I'll call. Thanks again, S.*

Barefoot, she went back into the living room. JoBeth was still asleep, snoring softly. Sara tucked the envelope into the spiral notebook, then checked the front door locks. The exhaustion was on her now, bone deep.

She went back to Danny's room, saw he hadn't moved. Then she went to her own, leaving the door open so she could hear him when he woke. She climbed under a single sheet, the room already bright, sunlight coming through the blinds. She thought about getting up to draw the curtains, but her body would not move.

When she closed her eyes she saw flashing red and blue lights, a dark form splayed out on wet grass. The head rose up, eyes fixed on her. Derek Willis looked at her and said, *Why?*

She rolled over, willed the vision away, pulled a second pillow close. She held it tight to her, arms wrapped around it. She slept and did not dream.

# TWO

Snow was swirling in the air — just flecks of it, only October still — when Morgan steered the old Monte Carlo onto Lyons Avenue. Rows of burned-out brownstones on both sides, abandoned and stripped cars. He passed an empty lot, saw two men standing around a fire in a fifty-five gallon drum. They watched as he drove past.

At the next corner, there was a makeshift shrine against a telephone pole. Flickering votive candles, a stuffed bear, a white T-shirt pinned to the pole. Something written on it, too far away to read.

He had the stereo on — Harold Melvin and the Blue Notes' "I Miss You," the long version — and he turned the sound down now, swung a right onto a side street. He slowed, watched the houses, the car's exhaust rumbling. The brownstone he wanted was ahead on the left; broken-down porch, weathered plywood over the big front windows.

He drove past slowly, taking in the barren front yard, the gang tags on the plywood. Hoped they didn't have a dog.

He went up a block, made a U-turn, and parked in front of an empty storefront. He switched the engine off, the big V8 quivering for a moment with pre-ignition, then going silent.

Watching the brownstone, he got the bottle of Vicodin from the pocket of his leather car coat. He was feeling the pain again, on his right side just below his ribs. It always came with stress. He shook a pill into his palm, broke it in two, put half on his tongue, and dry-swallowed it. He caught a glimpse of himself in the rearview, not liking what he saw. His face thinner, his hair grayer, the color of ash.

Time to get on with it. He put the half pill back, the bottle in his pocket, opened the door.

When he got out of the car, he felt the deep arthritic ache in his hips. This cold this early, it would be a rough winter. He locked the door, looked up and down the street, saw no one. The houses were all condemned, an urban renewal project that never happened. The only people in them would be squatters — fiends and smoke-hounds looking to get off the street as the weather turned.

Early afternoon and the sky a hard gray, his breath frosting in the air. He wore cotton work gloves, but his hands were still cold. As he walked toward the house, bits of glass crunched under his boots: crack vials, broken bottles. This part of the city was paved with them.

He stopped outside the brownstone. Three stories, a wealthy white man's house back in the day. The front yard was small and sloped, the stone steps that led up to the boarded-over door chipped and discolored. An extension cord ran from a second-floor window into the house next door.

He got the cell out, speed-dialed the number. Rohan answered on the first ring.

"Yo."

"It's Morgan. How do I get up in this place?"

"You early. Come around the side, man."

Morgan closed the phone, went around the house to the small side yard. A toppled birdbath lay broken in the weeds. There was a door there, and it opened as he approached. Standing inside was a chubby teenager — fourteen, fifteen — with a red North Face jacket, baggy jeans. Under the

29

jacket was a black T-shirt with red letters that said STOP SNITCHING. Morgan towered over him.

"You got a dog in there?"

"What?"

"Dog," Morgan said. "You got a pit in there or something?"

"No, man. No dog in here."

Morgan went past him into a big, bare kitchen, all the fixtures ripped out. The ceiling was sagging plaster, water-stained, ready to drop.

The boy locked the door behind them. Two dead bolts, a police bar that fit into a slot on the floor, all new.

"Hold on," the boy said.

Morgan turned, raised his arms. The boy reached under his coat, touched his sides, then around to the small of his back, knelt, patted his ankles. He ran his hands down the sides of the coat, felt the bottle of pills, took it out.

"What are these?"

"Those are mine," Morgan said.

The boy rattled the pills in the bottle, then dropped it back in Morgan's pocket. He nodded at a hallway. "Awright."

Morgan went down the hall, past a set of stairs with gaps in the railing. A series of linked heavy-duty extension cords snaked down the steps from above. Morgan followed them into the living room.

Rohan sat on an old couch in the center of the room, a scarred-up coffee table in front of him. He was hollowing out a cigar with a razor blade, a plastic bag of marijuana at his elbow. A floor lamp a few feet away was the only light. Next to it a space heater glowed red.

"You boys live here?" Morgan said to him. "You crazy."

Rohan didn't look up. He brushed tobacco onto the floor, packed marijuana into the blunt.

"No, man, this the shop," he said. "Just business here."

He was in his mid-twenties, wearing an identical North Face coat, a white basketball jersey underneath, black jeans, Timberlands. His hair hung long in braids. Morgan could see the three tattooed paws on the side of his neck. A chromed automatic rested on the cushion to his right.

The boy brushed past Morgan, went over to stand by the heater, the mantel of an old dead fireplace at his back. He stood wide-legged, arms crossed. Morgan could see the butt of the gun in his waist.

Rohan licked the edges of the blunt, pushed them together, surveyed his work, licked some more. He took a plastic lighter from the table and passed the flame back and forth over the wet edges to seal them.

"How old are you?" the boy said.

Morgan looked at him. "What do you care?"

"Just askin'."

"Morgan a player back in the day," Rohan said. "A straight-up OG." He looked up for the first time. "He be the Trouble Man back then. Like the movie." He looked at the boy. "You see that flick, Raj? Marvin Gaye music? Dude drive around in a Lincoln Continental, blowing up people's shit?"

"Nah." Raj shook his head.

Rohan fired the lighter, got the blunt going. He drew deep, held it out. Raj took it, hit off it, gave it back, the acrid smell of it filling the room. Rohan blew a long stream of smoke to the side, held the blunt in Morgan's direction. Morgan shook his head.

"This the chronic," Rohan said. "Not that weak-ass shit Mikey-Mike peddling these days."

"Where'd you get that from?" Morgan said.

Rohan shrugged, held the blunt out, and Raj took it again.

"Free market these days, yo," Rohan said. "If the product weak, if the price ain't right, people gonna go elsewhere. Everyone know Mikey's weed ain't been for real since the Colombians got busted. His coke and dope, too. And now he facing his own case. He scraping, and everyone on the street know it."

"That's temporary."

"Maybe. Maybe not. But he couldn't even make the re-up last time, if I remember correctly. Now I moved a lot of his shit when it was good, and we made mad money together, but things different now."

Raj handed the blunt back, and Rohan set it on the edge of the table.

"He knows all that," Morgan said. "He's working on it. He's making some moves, get the good stuff flowing again soon."

"When he do, we talk. If the shit's good, then we do business. If it ain't, we don't. That's the way things work."

"You two go way back," Morgan said. "Word gets around you're not with him anymore, it's bad for everyone."

"You talking about loyalty? It's about product, yo. Tough enough to make a living as it is, without slinging bad shit, taking people's money for it, expecting them to be happy because of who it came from. I've got a responsibility to my people, you know?"

"I understand. Mikey got a sample of the new stuff, wanted me to lay it on you."

Rohan looked at Raj, then back at Morgan. "Why you wait so long to tell me that?"

Raj laughed. "Yeah, lay it *on* us."

Morgan looked at him, and Raj met his eyes, didn't look away.

"Morgan still be talking that old-school jive," Rohan said, "but I follow. Like it is, brother. Like it *is*. Where the shit at?"

"In my car. Up the street. I'll give it to you, you try it. You like it, there's more coming. You don't, then that's that."

"You still got that hooptee? Cutlass or some shit?"

"Monte Carlo."

"You oughta shake some dollars loose from Mikey. Get yourself a new ride. That shit be out of style."

Morgan went back down the hall to the kitchen, saw a gray blur cross the floor and disappear into a doorless pantry. Rat.

Raj came up behind, started undoing the locks.

"Be back in a minute," Morgan said.

"Best be."

Morgan went through the side yard, down to the street. He walked the block to the Monte Carlo. Still no one in sight. He went around to the trunk. Raj watched from the

34

doorway.

Morgan keyed the trunk open, raised the lid so it shielded him. He took the Beretta from under an army blanket, the metal cold even through his gloves. He put the gun in his right-hand pocket, reached into the wheel well, and took out the paper lunch bag there. Inside was a plastic sandwich bag of marijuana. He slipped it into his left-hand pocket, shut the trunk.

More flurries now, wet and thick, the wind blowing them around. A sheet of newspaper flew along the gutter, wrapped itself around his leg. He pulled it loose, let the wind take it, walked back to the brownstone, hands in his pockets, feeling the weight of the gun.

The pain was gone now. He went up the walk and into the side yard. Raj stepped aside to let him through.

Morgan handed the plastic bag over. Raj took it, shut the door, worked the locks. He held the bag up, shook it. A gust of wind rattled the door.

"Looks like the same old shit to me," he said.

"Fire it up. See."

They went into the hall, Raj leading the way. Morgan let him get a few steps ahead, then took the Beretta from his pocket and said, "Yo."

The boy turned, saw the gun, and Morgan shot him twice in the chest, the noise loud in the narrow hallway. The impact bounced him off the wall, left blood there, and Morgan stepped around him as he fell, moved quickly into the living room.

Rohan was already up from the couch, the gun in his hand. Morgan shot him through the left shoulder. His legs tangled and he went down, clipping the edge of the table. The gun fell back onto the couch.

Morgan kicked the table away, held the Beretta on him. Rohan rolled onto his side, gasping. He lifted a hand as if to ward off another shot.

"Cash," Morgan said.

"Fireplace. Up in there. The stash, too."

Morgan went to the fireplace, still watching him. With his left hand, he reached up into the flue, felt material. He lifted until it came loose, drew it down and out. A canvas knapsack. It thumped on the floor when he dropped it.

"It's all in there, man," Rohan said. "Just take it."

Morgan knelt, unzipped it. Banded stacks of money, a G-pack of vials. He shook it all out onto the floor. Rohan lowered his hand, pressed it to his shoulder inside the coat, the white jersey turning red.

Morgan stood, pointed the Beretta at him, his finger on the curved trigger. He nodded at the couch. "If you're gonna reach for that piece, son, now's the time."

Rohan shook his head. "I ain't reaching for anything."

"All right, then," Morgan said, and fired three times. Casings hit the floor. Bits of insulation from Rohan's jacket floated in the air.

Morgan put the cash back in the knapsack, hefted it, left the G-pack on the floor. A reward for whoever found the bodies.

He decocked the Beretta, put it in his pocket, went around and picked up casings. He had to hunt for the last one, found it under the couch. He was breathing heavy by the time he was done.

When he was satisfied he'd left nothing behind, he went back out through the hallway, picked up the two casings there. Raj lay still, but there were red-flecked bubbles on his lips. Beneath the bloody T-shirt, his chest rose and fell in shallow breaths.

Morgan left him there, undid the locks on the kitchen door, closed it behind him. Wind pulled at him as he walked back to the Monte Carlo. The street still empty, he opened the trunk, dropped the knapsack inside, shut the lid. He unlocked the driver's side door, got behind the wheel.

As he pulled away from the curb, he turned the stereo up. The same song, Teddy Pendergrass singing to an ex-lover, telling her how he'd changed.

Morgan made a right onto Lyons, back toward downtown Newark. At the next intersection a crossing guard stepped out into the street. She wore an orange vest, blue uniform, carried a STOP sign.

He braked smoothly. The guard moved to the middle of the crosswalk, and the kids came across. Fourth, fifth grade maybe. Girls with ribbons in their hair, winter coats, pink vinyl knapsacks, the boys running ahead, laughing.

Last to cross was a girl no older than nine or ten. She turned and looked at Morgan, met his eyes through the windshield. Not smiling.

*Don't look at me like that, little girl,* he thought. *I know what I've done.*

The crossing guard hurried her along, smiled at Morgan. He raised a hand to her, drove on.

The snow was sticking now, the wind driving it against the windshield. He switched the wipers on, listened to them thump, turned the music louder, Teddy still pleading: *Miss you, miss you, miss you.*

# Three

She found him sitting at the bar at Tiger Tail's, a shot glass and Heineken in front of him, Johnny Cash's "Folsom Prison Blues" coming from the jukebox.

"You played that, didn't you?" she said.

He turned. "Hey, Sara."

She took the stool to his right. Althea the barmaid saw her, came over.

"Evening, Deputy Cross. Guinness?"

"Please."

Billy sipped from his beer, toyed with the empty shot glass.

"What was that?" Sara said.

"Peppermint schnapps."

"I didn't think anybody over sixteen drank that."

"Yeah, it's pretty awful. But it gets the job done."

Althea came back with the pint of Guinness. Billy pushed a wet twenty toward her. She took it, moved away.

"Hard to believe you're still on your feet," Sara said. "You get any sleep today?"

"A little."

Althea brought the change. The Guinness was colder than Sara liked, but dark and strong. For a while, she'd taken to black and tans, mixing it with a lighter beer. She drank little these days, though, and when she did she found she preferred the Guinness straight. It always surprised the men she met, the few she drank with.

"They give you a hard time this morning?" she said.

"Boone from the state attorney's, he's okay. Used to be a deputy down here, you know that?"

"No."

"Yeah, bottom of the ladder, just like you and me. Made his way up to undersheriff under Hammond. When Winston ran for state attorney, Hammond put a block of votes his way. Flip side was if he won, Winston had to take Boone. Before your time, I guess."

"He rewarding him or getting rid of him?"

"Maybe a little of both. Boone's a good man, he's just a little . . ." He took a sip of beer. "Ambitious. He and Elwood did the interview together. Videotape, the whole thing."

"Who's writing it?"

"Boone, I think."

"What'd he say?"

"That it looked like a clean shoot. What else could they say? It was. Part that bothers them is I was the only person there to say one way or another. At least the only one still breathing. They talk to you yet?"

"No," she said. "Elwood called me. I'm meeting them tomorrow. I won't have much to add, though, except what I saw when I got there."

"I'm sorry about that."

"About what?"

"That you had to be there, take the call. I didn't even know you were on."

"When you called it in, I was closest to your ten-twenty. I just wish I'd gotten there sooner. It might have gone a different way."

He looked at the clock over the bar. Almost ten. "Kind of late for you to be out, isn't it? Who's watching Danny?"

"JoBeth. I was worried about you. Figured I'd drive past just in case. Saw your truck."

She turned on her stool, looked around the bar. Two Mexicans — or Guatemalans more likely — playing pool in the alcove in the back. A couple of booths on the far wall were occupied. She saw Angie, the dispatcher, at one, with two men Sara didn't know, a pitcher of beer on the table between them. Angie was laughing, waving a cigarette. She caught Sara's eye, saw who she was with, and turned away again. *Great,* Sara thought. *Maybe coming here was a mistake after all.*

There were a handful of serious drinkers at the bar on either side of them, a couple of whom Sara recognized. She'd met most of the hardcore alcoholics in St. Charles County, either booking them for DWI or helping pull them out of their overturned pickups.

Billy signaled to Althea, pointed at his shot glass.

"How many of those you have?" Sara said.

"This is my third. Was my third, I mean."

"Better take it easy. You'll pay for it in the morning."

"I'm paying for it now."

Althea came down, poured from the bottle, took his money.

Billy raised his glass to Sara. From the jukebox came Warren Zevon's "Lawyers, Guns and Money."

"Now this, I *know* you played," she said.

"More than once." He sipped the schnapps. " 'Dad, get me out of this.' "

"Is Lee-Anne around? Maybe you ought to call her."

"She's down with friends in West Palm. She's coming back in a couple days."

"She know what happened?"

"She knows."

"And she's not coming back sooner?"

"Soon enough," he said and drank.

She sipped Guinness. In the mirror behind the bar she could see Angie in the booth, talking to the men but looking toward her every few minutes. Sara suddenly wanted to be somewhere else.

"So what happened?" Billy said. He'd turned to her.

"With what?"

"With us."

"Ah, Bill."

"It's one of the things I regret most, you know. Out of everything. Not being able to make it work."

"Let's not start this up again."

"I could have been better for you, I know. Sometimes I wish I could go back, figure out exactly when it was things started to go wrong."

"I don't know," she said. "Maybe about the time you started sleeping with Dolly Parton back there, what do you think?"

He looked over at Angie's booth.

"That was a mistake," he said.

"That supposed to make me feel better?"

"I'm sorry."

"Just leave it, Billy."

He emptied the shot glass, looked at her. She'd worn jeans and a long-sleeved Harley-Davidson T-shirt despite the heat, not wanting to send him the wrong signal if she found him. But he was appraising her openly now, more than he would have sober. For a moment, it made her feel good. She knew he would ruin it, though, and seconds later, he did.

"Are you seeing anybody?"

"Come on, Billy."

"It's a simple question, isn't it?"

"Somebody," she lied. "Off and on."

"Off and on? What's that mean?"

She drank Guinness, put the glass down.

"All you've been through," she said, "you really think this is the right time for that conversation?"

He rooted through the bills on the bar, pushed a five forward, folded the rest. "You're right. I think I need to get out of here."

When he got off the stool, he lost his balance for a moment, put one hand against the bar. "Leg's asleep."

She looked at him, feeling that familiar sensation. Years since she'd known it first-hand, but here it was again, stronger than

45

ever. Disappointment, almost resignation. *You always let me down, Billy Boy. Always. And you don't even know it.*

"Hold up," she said. "You get DWI'ed out there, how's that look for the review?"

"I'm okay."

"You're not. Even if you were, why take the chance?"

He looked at her, his eyes watery, the skin around them taut and red.

"You know I'm right," she said.

He raised his hands to shoulder height. Surrender.

"I'll drive you home," she said. "You can get your truck tomorrow."

She slid off the stool. Althea nodded to them.

"I've got to take a leak first," he said and went off to the men's room near the pool table, his walk unsteady. The two players looked at him for a moment, then went back to their game.

She waited by the front door. When he came back there was a wet spot on the front of his jeans. *Like a little kid.* When they first met, his childishness had appealed to her in some ways. Then it had begun to feel like just another burden.

She opened the door for him. Over her shoulder, she saw Angie in the booth, watching them as they went out.

It had rained briefly, and puddles in the dirt lot reflected the neon from the window signs. She'd parked under a southern pine near the edge of the lot. She got the keypad out, beeped the doors open.

"You need anything from your truck?" His black Ford F-150 pickup was parked nose first against the fence a few spots away.

He shook his head, followed her to the Blazer. She opened the driver's side door, waited until he got up in the passenger side without falling before she climbed up herself.

She started the engine. It coughed, hesitated.

"Needs a tune-up," he said.

"Doesn't like the wet weather."

"Points and plugs."

"Next paycheck, maybe."

She turned out of the parking lot, splashing through puddles.

"They oughta pave this," he said. "Make it not look so Florida white trash. Proud as I am of my own Florida white trashness."

She smiled at that, turned east on the county road, woods on both sides of them. He powered down his window, and she turned the air-conditioning off, slid her own window down a little.

They drove in silence for the first five minutes, headlights cutting a path through the night.

"You ever hear from Roy?" he said.

"You're the second person today to ask me that."

"So I guess the answer's no?"

"He's not coming back. Even if he was, I can't live my life worrying about it, wondering about it. Three years is a long time. If he was going to, he would have."

"Never could understand that."

"What part of it?"

"Leaving a woman like you."

"You mean a woman with a son?"

"That, too."

"I wonder about that myself," she said.

"Birthdays? Anything?"

She shook her head.

"You could find him if you want to. These days it isn't hard."

"Who says I want to? And what's with all the ancient history tonight?"

"Sorry," he said and sat back.

He was quiet for a while, and then he said, "You know what I can't get out of my mind?"

"What?"

"That car seat."

"Don't let it bother you so much," she

said. "A lot of times for a drug run, gun run, they'll put a car seat in the back. Makes them look less suspicious if they get stopped."

He picked up a plastic brontosaurus from the floor, looked at it, turned it over in his hands, put it back down.

"I don't know," he said. "I think that one was for real."

She saw the lights of his house up ahead, the red lens that marked the mailbox.

"With what you're making now," she said, "you could have moved closer to town a long time ago."

"Why would I do that? I like it out here. Reminds me of what I come from."

She made a right into the long dirt driveway, slowed to ease over the ruts and bumps. The house loomed up on the right. It was bordered by woods on two sides, on the other a long-dead cornfield. There was a carport in the sideyard, empty now, a dirt front yard, concrete steps leading up to the front door.

She pulled up, cut the headlights, left the engine running. It was the first time she'd been out here in two years. Light shone through the kitchen curtains. She remembered standing at that window, doing dishes he'd let pile up for days. She'd look out at the desiccated cornstalks, the woods beyond, grateful she didn't live here.

"Want to come in?" he said. "It's been a while."

"I don't think so."

He made no move to get out. She could hear crickets, the muffled hoot of an owl off in the trees.

"It's late," she said. "You should go inside."

"I know." He cocked his head slightly, a look that used to make her warm to him no matter what, and he knew it. He leaned close, and she didn't move away. Their lips met. He kissed her hard, and she let him at first, tasting the schnapps, let his tongue slide in, and then it all felt wrong, bad wrong, and she put a hand on his chest, pushed him away. He sagged back against the passenger side door.

"Sorry," he said.

"You don't need to apologize. But you need to go."

He opened the door. The courtesy light went on, and she could see the disappointment in his face and something else, despair even, or close to it.

He got out, turned to her.

"It's good to see you," he said. "I miss you sometimes."

"I miss you, too. Sometimes."

He smiled a little, and it made her feel better to see it. He shut the door, crossed around the front of the Blazer, tapped the hood twice as he started toward the house.

She watched him go up the steps, open the screen door, fit his key in the lock. He turned to wave to her, and she waved back. He shut the door behind him. Another light went on inside.

She sat that way for a few minutes, engine running, watching the house. Wondering if he would come back out, and what she would do if he did.

After a while, she backed up, swung around, turned the headlights on, and drove home.

# FOUR

The office had hard plastic chairs, joined together in groups of four. Morgan had been sitting for almost a half hour, sharing the room with a heavy woman, her crying baby, and an old white man with toothpick-thin arms and legs. There was a TV mounted high on the opposite wall, a soap opera playing without sound.

The receptionist had shut the window above her desk. Morgan could see her on the phone behind the pebbled glass. On his lap was a two-month-old *Newsweek*. He flipped through the pages, reading an item here and there, looking at the ads.

The door beside the desk buzzed, opened, and a short black woman in a white coat came out.

"Mr. Morgan?"

He took off his reading glasses, folded them and put them in a shirt pocket, and got up, his knees aching. He dropped the magazine on his seat. She held the door open, and he followed her down a hall to a treatment room.

"You can hang your coat there," she said, and he took the leather off, hung it on a peg on the back of the door. She weighed him on a scale, took his blood pressure, pulse, and temperature, noted them on a clipboard chart. She told him the doctor would be with him shortly, closed the door, and left him alone.

He sat on the treatment table, paper crinkling under him, looked around. There was a cutaway chart on one wall showing the progression of heart disease, cholesterol buildup in the arteries. Another had the seven warning signs of Type 1 diabetes.

After a few minutes, the door opened and a tall, skinny white man came in. Midthirties, short blond hair, glasses.

"I'm Dr. Kinzler." He put out his hand. Morgan shook it. "Dr. Rosman at the clinic sent over your file this morning."

He picked up Morgan's chart from the counter, looked at it, flipped pages.

"You saw Dr. Rosman last week?" he said without looking up.

"Tuesday." It was the first he'd spoken.

"You know you're down five pounds from then?"

Morgan shook his head. He was worried it would be more.

"Vitals are fine, temperature normal." He set the chart down. "Any pain?"

Morgan touched the right side of his stomach. "Here, sometimes."

Kinzler felt there, probed gently.

"Liver size seems normal," he said, "but we'll run some more blood work."

He slid the chestpiece of his stethoscope up beneath Morgan's sweater, the metal cold, asked him to breathe deep. He did the same in back, between his shoulder blades.

"How long with the pain?" he said.

"Three, four weeks. Bad the last week or two."

"You taking anything for it?"

"Vicodin when I need it. Try not to take it unless I have to."

"Good."

He made notes on the chart and then stepped back and leaned against the counter, clipboard held in crossed arms.

"So you know about the other test results, the second biopsy?" he said. "Dr. Rosman discussed them with you?"

"A little."

"Goblet cell carcinoid is fairly rare. It only strikes one in about a hundred thousand people. And it can be fairly unpredictable.

We don't know a lot about it yet, but there are some relatively standard ways of treating it. You're . . ." He looked at the clipboard. "Fifty-seven?"

"Fifty-eight. Next month."

"You're in good shape for your age. Fit. That'll help. But a lot of this — and what we decide to do — will depend on how early we caught it. That's why we'll do a full set of blood work today. Then we can discuss how to proceed. Have you had an MRI or CAT scan?"

Morgan shook his head.

"You have insurance?"

"No."

"Medicare, Medicaid, anything?"

"No."

"That's an issue. There's a range of treatments that might be required, once we figure out which way to go."

"I can get the money. I'll do what I need to do."

"What line of work are you in, Mr. Morgan?"

He shifted on the table. "Handyman, construction, whatever I can get."

"Construction, huh? Union?"

"No."

"Pension?"

Morgan shook his head.

"There's various things you can apply for," Kinzler said. "Social aid, some elder programs you might be able to get in on. All of it's worth looking into. You're likely eligible for Medicaid as well."

"I'll pay what I have to pay."

"You seem confident."

Morgan shrugged.

"Either way," Kinzler said, "we can't waste much time. We have to be proactive with these types of cancers. They removed the appendix when?"

"August."

"So it probably took at least a couple weeks for the initial biopsy results to come back. Did you have any symptoms before that?"

"No. I had the pain, I went to the clinic. They sent me to the hospital."

"That's one of the ways goblet cell presents," Kinzler said. "Or at least one of the ways we catch it. Routine appendectomies, and if they find a tumor in the removed organ, bingo. There you are."

"What are you saying?"

"I'm saying early is better. And we might be fairly early here, which is good news. Depending on how far it's gotten, where it's spread, surgery may be an option as well. We go in, take out as many of the tumors as

we find. Afterward, we put you on a mainte-
nance diet of chemo, maybe radiation, if it
looks like it'll be effective. Then we test you
regularly, see if they come back."

The woman came back in, carrying a kit
she opened on the counter.

Kinzler put out his hand. "Doris will draw
some blood. We'll get back to you when we
know more."

"That's it?"

"For now." He kept his hand out until
Morgan shook it. "At least a few days before
we know anything. Then we'll set you up
for a scan. You're not going anywhere,
right?"

"No," Morgan said. The woman had a
plastic syringe out, cartridges, a blue rubber
strap.

"I'll leave you in good hands, then, Mr.
Morgan. We'll speak soon." He shut the
door behind him.

The woman tugged at the left sleeve of his
pullover. He rolled it up, and she tied the
strap around his upper arm and swabbed
the crook of his elbow with an alcohol pad.
When he made a fist, the veins rose in his
forearm. She laid the needle tip on the
thickest one, and he winced as the steel slid
in.

An empty plastic cartridge went into the

syringe. She pressed it home, and he watched dark red blood swirl into the tube, slowly fill it. His blood. His life.

He waited in the doorway of a beauty supply shop, its metal grille covered with graffiti. Eleven P.M. and only a handful of cars had passed in the half hour he'd been there. In the distance, the Prudential Building rose over the skyline like a floodlit tombstone. No matter where you went in the city, it was always in sight.

He watched the big black Chevy Suburban come down the street slow. Tinted windows, silver rims and spinners. He stepped out of the doorway, and the Suburban swung to the curb, the rear passenger door opening. He got in, and C-Love pulled the door shut behind him.

The Suburban had been customized with two facing bench seats. Mikey-Mike sat in the rear one, arms up on the seatback. Morgan slid onto the other, facing him. C-Love settled in beside him, close to the door. They pulled away from the curb, hip-hop throbbing low from hidden speakers.

Mikey wore a Michael Jordan jersey, an Adidas headband, and warm-up pants and jacket, but he was pushing three fifty, and Morgan doubted if he'd seen a basketball court in twenty years. There was a thick rope of gold around his neck. To Morgan, it was all foolish gangsta bling that said *Drug dealer. Lock my ass up.*

Morgan wore his leather, the Beretta tucked into his belt in back. He looked behind him, saw the Coleman twins, Dante at the wheel, DeWayne riding shotgun, a hundred pounds heavier than his brother, with a lazy left eye. He was a month out of Rahway at most. He looked at Morgan without expression.

"Yo, DeWayne," Mikey said. "Turn that shit down."

The music faded to a dull thumping Morgan could feel through the seat. He looked out the window. They drove past City Hall with its gold-leaf dome, marble steps, barricades in front.

"That was good work you put in," Mikey said.

"True that," C-Love said. "Showed those niggas the error of their ways."

"But I heard some things," Mikey said.

"Like what?" Morgan said.

"Like maybe that bitch had a stash there."

Morgan reached into his pockets. He felt C-Love stiffen, turn toward him. Morgan took out banded stacks of cash, tossed them onto the seat beside Mikey.

"There was shit there, too," Morgan said. "I left it."

"Why?"

"Too much trouble. A whole G-pack. I wasn't going to carry it around."

Mikey looked at the stacks, then at C-Love. "Count that shit," he said. C-Love leaned over, picked up the bills.

"There's seven there," Morgan said. "I found fourteen, kept half."

C-Love finished counting, nodded. Mikey leaned forward, took one of the banded thousand-dollar stacks, tossed it into Morgan's lap.

"Don't ever trust anyone who's not taking his share," Mikey said. He looked at C-Love. "If a nigga ain't stealing a little, he's stealing a lot."

Morgan left the stack where it was.

"Maybe you need it more than me," he said.

"Nah," Mikey said. "What those lawyers are charging, that wouldn't buy them lunch. Take it, 'cause we got something else to talk about, too."

Morgan put the money away. "What?"

"That deal down south," Mikey said. "Some shit happened. Ain't gotten to the bottom of it yet."

"Maybe you should back off it."

60

"It's not that easy. I need that connect, the money it's gonna bring in, to pay those motherfuckers working my case. They got another delay, but first of the year, man, they can't put that shit off anymore."

"What happened?"

"Don't know. I sent someone down there, prime the pump, get things moving, but he never made it. People he was supposed to meet called, said 'What the fuck?' I didn't know what to tell them."

"What was he carrying?"

"We'll talk about that shit someplace else. But I may need you to go down there soon."

"Why?"

"Find out what the fuck happened. And who's responsible. And settle that shit before it gets out of hand."

Morgan thought about Kinzler, what he'd said.

"I got some things going on," he said, "I need to take care of. Up here."

"Ain't no shit that can't wait. I'm waiting to hear back on something. When I do, might be I'm gonna holler at you. And you need to be ready to go."

Morgan looked out the window, felt them watching him. The Suburban rolled past a block-long housing project.

"What?" Mikey said. "You actually need

to think on this? Whatever it is, I'll make it worth your while. You know me."

"Yeah," Morgan said. "I know you."

"Besides, being gone for a while might be a good thing, case someone's thinking payback for that work you done, you feel me?"

"I'll handle it if they do."

"I know you will. Just sayin'."

"Up at the corner's fine."

"Dante," Mikey said, "pull up over there by the playground."

The Suburban rolled to a stop.

"Well?" Mikey said.

Morgan reached across for the door latch, popped it.

"Call me," he said and got out.

He walked home down Washington Street, past boarded-up tenements, vacant lots between them like missing teeth. At the corner of West Kinney, he stopped in front of an empty brownstone, windows bricked up, the facade darkened with smoke damage. A sign in the yard promised new condominiums to come, gave a phone number.

He'd lived there for six years, from the time his grandmother died until he'd turned fifteen and taken to the streets. A group home, him and ten other boys. Back in 1967, on the second day of the riots, he'd snuck up to the roof, watched smoke and flames bloom from the corner of Springfield and Bergen. Sirens everywhere, and the crack of gunfire blocks away. Gray ash had fallen from the sky like snow, covering the city. A lifetime ago.

He walked on.

# FIVE

The hill. It was always the hill that killed her.

Sara ran hard, her legs like lead, eyes on the road ahead, the top of the hill. She was waiting for the pain to stop, for the bliss of oxygenated blood to take over, but it hadn't. Just more pain and more hill, the sound of her breathing and the noise of her sneakers on the blacktop.

Counting the paces now, distracting herself from the pain, and then she was up, at the top, the road long and straight in front of her. She resisted the temptation to slow. Engine noise behind her. She moved farther up on the shoulder, kicking up pine needles as she ran. An empty flatbed truck went past, Howie Twelvetrees from the municipal garage at the wheel. He blew the horn, and she waved to him without breaking stride.

Ahead was the creek, the wooden bridge, her turnaround point. She crossed it, sneakers thumping on the wood, then circled to the other side of the road, started back. One mile up, one mile back.

Downhill she had to watch her speed or risk taking a header onto the pavement. When she reached the bottom, she slowed, breathing hard but knowing the worst was over.

She thought about her interview with Elwood and Boone that morning. It had been shorter than she'd expected, less than a half hour. No, she hadn't heard the shots. Yes, Billy had told her what had happened. No, she had no reason to believe it had gone any other way.

The questions touched only briefly on their relationship, and Boone had seemed almost embarrassed about it. Still, the sheriff had been right. In Hopedale everyone knew your business.

She slowed when the house came in sight, breathing deeper, filling her lungs. She saw the front door open and Danny come out on the steps to meet her, JoBeth behind him. Sara felt the smile come to her face unbidden. She lifted her arm in a weary wave.

A half hour later she was showered, dressed in jeans and sweatshirt, Danny on her lap.

After JoBeth had left, they'd filled the bird feeders in the backyard, fed and watered the rabbits.

There were four of them, kept in a hutch she'd made from scrap lumber and chicken wire. He'd named them after cartoon characters — Bugs, Wile E., Daffy, Yosemite. It pleased and worried her. He'd grown close to them, and she knew someday they'd go out to feed them and there would be only three, or fewer if a dog got into the hutch. It would be his first experience with death, something she wanted to postpone as long as possible.

Now they were reading a book of Aesop's fables, one they'd read a half-dozen times before. He knew it by heart. She was always surprised how fast he learned, how he forgot nothing.

She felt warm, relaxed, had tried to put last night's awkwardness with Billy out of her mind. She felt centered here, in her house, Danny's reassuring weight on her lap. This was where she belonged. This was where she was strong.

She saw the fresh mark on his forearm then, hoped it was juice, Magic Marker maybe. She brushed at it. It was another bruise.

"How'd you get this?"

"I don't know. I bumped into something. Can I watch TV now?"

"Only for a little while, while I'm making dinner. It goes off when we sit down at the table. You know the rules."

"Okay," he said and tumbled off her lap, got the remote from the coffee table. He flicked it on, and the TV glowed into life. He stretched out on the carpet, legs kicked up behind him.

She got up, set the book on the table.

"Halloween's coming soon," he said.

"I know." They'd had this discussion before.

"I'm not sure what I want to be yet."

She looked at him. He didn't turn.

"Danny, we talked about this, remember? I know you want to go trick-or-treating, but I don't think it's such a good idea."

"Why not?"

"Because of how tired you get. Because you're sick, and being outside that long isn't good. All those reasons and more."

"All the other kids are going."

"Well, you're not all the other kids."

He was silent then, staring rapt at the cartoon blaring from the television. As she entered the kitchen he said, "Mom?"

"Yeah, kiddo?"

"How did I get sick?"

She stopped in the doorway, looked back at him. He hadn't looked away from the TV.

"I don't know, Danny. No one knows. It just happens."

"I'm tired of it."

"I know." She came back into the living room, sat cross-legged beside him, touched his thinning hair. He didn't respond. She leaned close, kissed the top of his head. "We'll get you well," she said. "I promise."

"Do you?"

"Yeah, baby, I do."

She got up then, turned away, not wanting him to see her cry.

In the kitchen she got a pan down from the cabinet, hamburger meat from the refrigerator. The sound of cartoons filled the kitchen as she busied herself, set the pan on the stove, got the heat on. Focusing on what she was doing, shutting everything else out of her mind. The patties sizzled as they met the pan.

"Mom?" he called from the living room.

"Yeah, hon?"

"I'm not a baby, you know. Not anymore."

She laughed, used the back of her hand to wipe her eyes.

"I know, Danny," she said. "I know."

Monday at noon, she drove out to Billy's

house. For no reason she could name, she took the long way, across the freight tracks and into the Libertyville section of town. Big Victorian houses, most in disrepair, some boarded up. She passed tree-shrouded overgrown yards, a street-corner Baptist church.

The neighborhood had been founded by freed slaves after the Civil War and had once boasted a flourishing black business district, a response to the segregation in the rest of Hopedale. But neither history nor architecture had been enough to keep people here. Most of the houses she saw were condemned or for sale. No gentrification here, just a neighborhood left to die, families moving out the first chance they got. Driving through now, she couldn't blame them.

She caught the county road, took it southwest. Once she passed the old drive-in, there was nothing but farms and fields. Ten minutes later, she turned down Billy's driveway, pulled the cruiser up behind his truck in the front yard. Lee-Anne's old Camaro was parked in the carport. Sara sat there for a moment, wondering if she should turn around, go back. *Since when have you let that bitch scare you off?*

She got out of the cruiser, switched on the handheld radio at her belt, plugged in the shoulder mike. *No calls yet today. Finally catching a break.*

She went up the steps, knocked on the screen door. She could hear music inside, reggae. She knocked again, heard noises, then the inside door opened. Lee-Anne looked at her through the screen.

"It's you," she said.

"I came to check on Billy. See how he was doing. It's my lunch break."

Lee-Anne looked past her to where the cruiser was parked. She wore a sleeveless black Jack Daniel's T-shirt, breasts loose under it, nipples visible through the material. Her long blond hair was braided and beaded on one side, and she wore low-slung jeans that showed an inch of skin, a navel ring. A barbed-wire tattoo circled her left upper arm.

"This police business?" she said.

"No."

"Billy," she said without turning, "that woman's here."

Sara looked past her into the living room, saw clothes on the floor, smelled the sweet tang of marijuana. Lee-Anne didn't move.

"You're looking butch these days," Lee-Anne said. "That uniform and all. That ain't no way to get a man, pretending to be one.

Though I guess there's some might like that."

Sara felt the heat in her face.

"I'll be outside," she said and went back down the steps.

She was standing by the cruiser when Billy came down, tucking a white T-shirt into jeans. He looked happy to see her.

"Hey, girl. I thought you were staying home today."

"Sheriff offered, but I turned him down."

"Why in hell would you do that?"

*You wouldn't understand, Billy. You never did.*

"People would talk," she said. "Say I was getting special treatment."

"Bullshit. Nobody's ever given you any special treatment. If they did you wouldn't take it anyway."

He got a pack of gum from his pocket, offered her a stick. She shook her head. He took a piece, rolled the wrapper up, and flicked it away.

"You drop a specimen?" she said.

"What, for Elwood? Yeah, soon as Boone got there. Why?"

"Was it clean?"

"Sure. Why do you ask?"

She lifted her chin at the house.

"That's just Lee-Anne," he said. "Can't

71

get her to stop. She doesn't do it too much these days, though."

"Secondhand smoke can make you test positive, too."

"It's not a problem, Sara. What's up?"

"Just came by. See how you were doing."

He shrugged, leaned back against the cruiser. "Sheriff wants me to see a counselor, man works for the county."

"Probably a good idea."

"I may not have a choice, the way Hammond puts it."

"Even better," she said. "Keeps you from having to make the decision yourself."

"And that's a good thing?"

"Sometimes."

He looked away, squinted. "Elwood called me a little while ago," he said.

"About what?"

"He told me you'd been in there. That your story matched up."

"Why wouldn't it?"

"I don't know. You never know what people are going to say in those situations."

"You've got nothing to worry about," she said. "I talked to the sheriff again this morning. He said there's still some paperwork to do, but it looks like they're going to rule it a clean shoot."

"He really say that?"

She nodded.

He blew air out, seemed to sink back against the cruiser, letting it take his weight.

She looked up, saw Lee-Anne at the kitchen window, watching them. "I don't think she likes me very much," she said.

"Lee-Anne? Well, you know the way that goes. It's a woman thing, I guess."

"I guess," Sara said. She got her keys out. "I need to get going, run by the market while I've got time."

"Thanks for coming by."

They stood there a moment, the silence awkward between them. Her radio crackled.

"Eight-seventeen?" Laurel, the day dispatcher. "Eight-seventeen?"

Sara keyed her shoulder mike.

"Eight-seventeen here."

"Eight-seventeen, please respond to Bell Hardware, Tupelo and Main, for possible shoplifter. Units already on scene."

"Responding," she said. "Ten-four. Out." She looked at him. "Gotta go. That's what passes for major crime around here. Guess I won't make it to the market after all."

The screen door opened. Lee-Anne stood there, arms folded.

"Looks like you've got to go, too," Sara said.

Billy looked back toward the house. "Then

I better," he said. Looked at her again. "It was nice last night," he said. "Seeing you again. Outside work. Felt like old times."

"I know," she said. "It did."

He started toward the house. Lee-Anne disappeared inside. He went up the steps, stopped, and looked back at the cruiser. Sara paused, the driver's door open. He looked at her for a long moment, then went in. Lee-Anne spoke to him — Sara could see their outlines through the screen — then caught the edge of the inner door and slammed it shut.

It was a little after five when she got back to the Sheriff's Office. She left the cruiser in the garage, turned in her keys and paperwork. As the only female deputy, there was no locker room for her to use. She either changed in the ladies' room or went home in uniform.

In the bathroom, she ran water in the sink, looked at herself in the mirror, thought about what Lee-Anne had said. *That ain't no way to get a man.*

She washed her hands and face, then changed into street clothes — jeans and black T-shirt, boots. She untied her hair, let it fall. Her uniform went into the tac bag along with the Kevlar vest, her shoes, and the rest of her equipment, the holstered Glock on top.

Back out in the corridor, she slung the bag over her shoulder, checked her mailbox. Reed, the ancient black janitor, was mopping the floor, pushing a yellow plastic bucket on wheels. He nodded at her as he went past.

In her mailbox was the direct deposit stub from her last paycheck. She tore the tabs away to check the hours and amount. Behind her, she heard the men's room door open.

"I thought you worked here just for the love."

Clay Huff came up beside her, wiping his hands on a paper towel. He was freshly showered and shaved for his shift, doused with cologne.

"Evening, Deputy," she said.

"Always so formal, Sara. Even after all this time. That ain't right."

When she turned from the mailboxes he was blocking her way. He was younger than her, a head smaller, but heavily muscled. When word had gotten around the Sheriff's Office that Roy had left her, he'd hit on her relentlessly for almost a year. It had only stopped when she started seeing Billy.

"Like your hair," he said. "You do something different with it?"

"Like what?"

"I don't know. Lightened it or something."

Another deputy brushed past them into the men's room. She folded her pay stub, slipped it into a pocket of the tac bag.

"Not really," she said, "and I didn't realize you were paying so much attention to my personal appearance."

He smiled, stepped back. "Just trying to be friendly. Compliment a colleague."

"Thanks."

"And I thought maybe with everything that's going on, you might want to have a drink, talk things out."

"I don't think so."

"Let me give you my number, case you change your mind."

"You never give it a break, do you?"

"No idea what you mean," he said.

She moved past him down the hall, knew he was watching her hips. When she got to the front, Laurel, the dispatcher, was motioning to her from her elevated desk.

Sara raised an eyebrow. Laurel cocked a finger at her, put the same finger to her lips.

When Sara went over, Laurel pointed at the sheriff's closed door.

"She's been in there more than an hour," she said. "She just showed up in a cab outside."

Through the glass, Sara could see a young black woman, late twenties, sitting across from the sheriff. He was leaning forward in his seat, elbows on his knees, talking to her. There was a suitcase beside her chair.

"Who's that?" Sara said.

"I only know who she says she is."

Sara looked at her. "What's that mean?"

"You know that man that got shot the other night? Willis?"

"What about him?"

"She says she's his wife."

# Six

Morgan lay on his bed, drew deeply from the joint. Eyes closed, he held the smoke inside, let it out slowly. A boom box on the bureau played low, a *Best of the Delfonics* cassette. After a while the pain in his stomach began to fade.

He was almost out of Vicodin, didn't want to go back into them tonight. He kept a small stash of reefer in the room but only smoked at night, when he was alone and the pain grew too much. Then he would double-lock the door, the Beretta on the nightstand, let the smoke carry him away.

He pinched the roach out, set it in the nightstand ashtray, felt himself slipping into sleep. When he woke, he could hear the muffled thump of music from the club across the street. He went to the window, looked out. A man stood on the corner below, cell phone to his ear. A dark BMW with tinted windows was parked half a block down.

Morgan had lived in this residential hotel for five years, paid seven hundred in cash every month and another hundred on top of that to the manager, to let him know if anyone came around or asked about him. He'd installed his own dead bolts in the door, kept the only keys. His second-floor room looked out over the front entrance, which was why he'd chosen it. From the window, he could see anyone coming or going from the building.

His mouth was dry, cottony, but he was hungry, too. There was a sink in one corner of the room, and he ran water, waited for it to clear, and then drank from the faucet, spit it out, and drank more. He got his cell out — thirty minutes left and he would toss it, buy another — and called in an order to the Chinese restaurant down the block.

His was one of the few rooms with its own bathroom — a toilet and shower stall in a space no larger than a closet, the door barely clearing the seat. Morgan stripped, looked at himself in the mirror. His stomach was loose and sagging, had once been rippled with muscle. His chest hair was mostly gray, a few shiny black ones still hiding in there. He touched his scars. The keloid near his left shoulder where he'd been shot in 1988, the year the crack wars had hit the city. The puckered flesh below his right nipple from being shanked in the chow line at Rahway. Low on his right side, the most recent one, a three-inch mark where they'd removed his appendix.

He showered, dressed, put on the leather coat, the Beretta under it in back. He went out, locked the door behind him. The stairwell smelled of mold and stale fried food. The lobby was empty, no one behind the bulletproof glass at the registration desk. That bothered him.

At the front door, he scanned the street. The man with the cell was gone. The BMW, too.

He went outside, the air cold and clear, crossed the street, and headed up the block to Halsey. He kept the Monte Carlo in a parking garage two blocks away, paid another hundred and fifty a month for that, but he used the car only when he had to.

He turned right at the corner. The restaurant was the only lit storefront on the block, the front windows steamed. Two teenagers stood outside talking on cell phones, wearing puffy coats, long white T-shirts, baggy jeans. One cut a look at Morgan as he crossed the street, then went back to his conversation.

A handful of tables inside, all empty. The Asian woman behind the register — she could have been twenty-five or fifty-five, he couldn't tell — put his bagged food on the counter without speaking. He paid her, waved off the change, the same ritual every time.

The bag was warm against his left side as he went out. His stomach rumbled with hunger. The teenagers were gone, the street empty. He looked up toward the corner of Halsey. A police car passed by, going fast.

He crossed the street in the opposite direction from which he'd come, taking the long way back. He cut across a vacant lot and into the narrow alley that ran behind it. Abandoned warehouses here, loading docks with graffiti-covered metal gates. A rat scuttled out of an overturned trash can, ran from him along the alley wall.

He stopped a few feet into the alley, turned to listen. Nothing. Kept going.

After two blocks, the alley grew wider. Now it ran behind a row of old houses with small bare yards, low wooden fences. He'd walk up to Mulberry, make a right, double back to the hotel.

He heard the noise then, a slight scuffing far behind him, back by the warehouses.

To his right was a house, the back window lit. A white sheet hung from a clothesline strung between dead trees. He stepped over the fence into the shadows of the yard, moved behind the sheet. There were cutout Halloween decorations in the window: a cat with an arched back, a jack-o'-lantern.

The noise again, then a low voice. The chirp of a cell phone being used as a walkie-talkie.

He set the bag on the ground, got the Beretta out, held it at his side. The chirp again, then silence. He waited.

Five minutes later, the man came up the alley after him, into the light wash from the back window. He wore a black watch cap, baggy denim. Morgan saw the three tattooed dog paws on the side of his neck.

The man looked at the house, then back the way he'd come. Morgan could see the automatic in his right hand. The other held the cell. He lifted it to his face. It chirped. He spoke low.

"Nah, man. He gone. He must be out on Mulberry by now. Bring the car around." He clicked the phone shut, looked at the house.

Morgan followed his glance. There was a boy — nine or ten at most — looking out the window, his arms folded on the sill. He watched the man without expression.

Black Cap lowered the gun so it was hidden at his side. He said, "Hello, little man," and then Morgan stepped out from behind the sheet, raised the Beretta, and shot him through the head.

He fell without a sound, the quick spinal looseness of instant death. Morgan stepped over the fence, looked back down the alley the way he'd come. There was a figure there, moving toward him, an outline against the streetlights at the far end. Morgan raised the Beretta, fired, heard the bullet whine off pavement. The figure leaped, hit and hugged the ground. Morgan turned and ran.

Mulberry was in sight, a block ahead. He headed for it, pain in his chest, and then the BMW screeched to a halt at the alley entrance, half on the sidewalk. He saw the back driver's side window roll down, the shotgun barrel come out. He fired at it twice, heard bullets punch metal, break glass.

There was a gap between the front bumper and the alley wall. He made it through, ran across Mulberry toward an empty lot, heard the engine roar, tires squeal behind him.

Another alley here, close walls and cracked blacktop. He ran, tripped, went down hard, the Beretta flying from his hand, skittering across the ground.

He lay on the blacktop, out of breath, the pain an iron band around his stomach and sides. The far end of the alley was about thirty feet ahead. He looked toward it but could not move. He looked behind him, back down the alley to the street beyond. The BMW was gone.

He sucked in air, felt the pain in his chest, rolled onto his side. His left palm was bloody where he'd tried to break his fall. Bits of gravel were embedded in the skin.

He got to his feet, looked around until he found the Beretta. He shuffled toward it, one hand on the wall for support. When he bent to pick it up, dizziness swept over him. He leaned against the wall until it ended. He could hear distant sirens.

When he reached the end of the alley, the street was empty. Still breathing hard, he waited in the shadows. A cab went past slow, stopped at a light. He slipped the Beretta into his right-hand coat pocket, stepped out into the street.

Morgan sat in the Monte Carlo, the Beretta on the seat beside him, the pain like a hot coal in his stomach.

He was parked a block down from his hotel, could see the BMW just around the corner up ahead, exhaust curling from its tailpipe, waiting.

He got his cell out, speed-dialed.

C-Love answered. "Yo."

"I have a situation here. I can't go back to my place."

Silence for a moment.

"Where you at?"

"That doesn't matter. What matters is I need a place to go."

"I hear you. Hold on."

When C-Love came back on he said, "Big Man says he can fix you up. You driving?"

"Yeah."

"Know that motel by the airport, one we party at sometimes?"

"I know it."

"He gonna call ahead, get a room for you. You go there, park around the back. Manager gonna give you the key, ain't gonna say anything else. You hang there till one of us call you back. You need anything?"

Morgan thought about what he'd left in the room. Some clothes, his pills, the boom box, about half his tapes. The others were in the car. The cash he'd taken from Rohan and the thousand Mikey had given him were in a safe deposit box at his bank, with the rest of his money. He had nothing else.

He looked at the BMW.

"Nah," he said. "I'm good."

"See you there, then," C-Love said and ended the call.

Morgan closed the cell, then started the engine, U-turned away from the curb. He watched the BMW in his rearview. It didn't move.

He switched on the stereo, the cassette player clicking on. Walter Jackson singing that his ship was coming in. He turned it louder. Drove with one hand on the gun.

# SEVEN

The sheriff was at the coffee station, with a mug that bore the eagle, globe, and anchor of the Marine Corps. Sara had just come on duty, hadn't picked up her keys yet.

"Who was that?" she said.

He looked at her. "Who?"

"That woman yesterday."

He sipped coffee.

"Need to talk to you about that," he said. "Come on in."

She followed him into the office.

"Close the door."

He stood at the window, sipped from the steaming mug, looked out. The flag was popping in the wind, the metal lanyard clanging against the pole.

"I guess I shouldn't have been surprised," he said.

"About what?"

He gestured at the chair across from his desk. She sat.

"That woman's name is Simone James," he said, "and she claims to be Derek Willis's wife, if not in a strictly legal manner. She says they have a child together. A three-year-old boy. She showed me pictures."

"What's she doing here?"

He put the mug down, sat. "Collect the body, when it's ready to be released. Ostensibly at least. Raise hell, most likely, is what I think."

"What did you tell her?"

"That we were conducting a full investigation. That it appeared to be a case of justifiable use of lethal force. She says Willis never carried a gun in his life. Wouldn't know what to do with one."

"He had one that night. More than one."

"That's what I told her. And his prints were on the .38. She didn't seem to buy it. I gave her Boone's number, the ME's, too. She'll call them, I expect. Get a lawyer, too, if she hasn't already. Being as you were a witness, you should be prepared."

"Everything I saw is in that report."

"I know, but she might want to talk to you. That's my read on her, at least, from my brief exposure. And you're not going to do that, right?"

"Of course not."

"If it comes down to a suit, lawyers and a

deposition, we'll talk to the FOP attorney, see what he says. Until then, we don't do anything. I've promised her access to the basic reports, but that's it. She's a cool customer, though."

"What do you mean?"

"I expected her to come in here with guns blazing, call us all a bunch of racists at least. Instead she asked her questions, and when I gave her answers, she asked more. Wasn't too forthcoming when it came to my own questions, though."

"Like what?"

"The car that Willis was driving was registered to a Wendell Abernathy, remember? Turns out Mr. Abernathy is seventy-five years old and hasn't renewed his driver's license in six years."

"What did she say to that?"

"She said it doesn't matter. She's right."

"Anything else turn up in the car?"

He shook his head, sipped coffee.

"What was in the overnight bag I saw?"

"Clothes. We put a drug dog on the car, too. No hits."

"Doesn't mean anything."

"You're right."

"So she asks around a little bit, maybe blows off some steam, then goes back to New Jersey."

*Or stays here and causes trouble for all of us.*

"Maybe, maybe not," he said. "We'll see. I've been going over those reports again, though."

"And?"

"There are a couple things that bother me. Boone and Elwood didn't think they were an issue, but I'm not so sure."

"What?"

"Billy says Willis was speeding, driving erratically, that he pulled him over because of that."

"So?"

"So he's already maybe a little nervous, doesn't know what he's getting into. New Jersey plates, that road, that time of night, no one else around. He knew something was up when he pulled that car over."

"I don't understand."

"Unusual situation. Remote location. SOP would have been to call it in, sit there and wait for backup before approaching the car. Instead, he calls it in and then gets out, engages the driver. And things get crazy."

"The way it happens sometimes."

"I know. But most deputies in a shooting situation — especially if they've never been in one before — will end up emptying their magazines, out of panic, instinct. They fire at the threat until it's eliminated. Billy only fired three times — just enough to do the job — and all of them in center body mass. Pretty good shooting for a man in fear of his life."

"You're blaming him because he didn't panic?"

"Not at all. Just another wrinkle in this thing. Something else to keep it from being as simple as it should."

"What else?"

He put the cup down.

"Why'd Willis run?" he said.

"Because he didn't want to go to jail."

"He'd be facing a gun charge, sure, but he'd be out on bail in a day or so. With a decent lawyer he might even beat the case, being as it wasn't his car in the first place. But he had no warrants, wasn't a fugitive. Why get into a gun battle with a deputy?"

"Maybe he was the one that panicked."

"Maybe. I just wish the whole thing made more sense."

She thought about what she'd told Billy at his house, how the sheriff was convinced it was a clean shoot. The relief in his face.

"I need to get out on the road," she said.

"I know. And I'm sure I don't need to remind you, Sara, but don't talk to anyone about this — *anyone* — without a lawyer from the county or the FOP present. That includes Billy."

"He's a fellow deputy. He's having a hard time with all this. How can you say —"

"Trust me, it's for the best. Now, I know you feel bad about what he's going through, you want to support him. I understand that. I do, too. But you need to be careful."

"It sounds like you're expecting the worst."

"I always expect the worst. It might be a good idea to stay away from him in general until all this gets cleared up."

*There it is. What you were waiting for.*

"I don't —"

He raised his hand. "I'm just saying. You need to keep in mind, someday you may be sitting in this chair instead of me."

"I don't know about that."

"I do, and that may come sooner than you think. If you want it, that is. In the meantime, you need to stay clear of things that could come back to haunt you later on."

"What do you mean?"

He sat back, looked at her. "This is going to sound cold," he said. "And maybe it is. But if things go bad on this, I don't want you catching any of it. You might be in an awkward position, because of that past situation — and because you were out there the night of the shooting. If someone has to take the hit on this, I want you well clear of it, for your own sake."

She watched him, waited for more.

"I tell you about when I was with the Rough Riders?" he said. "Running supplies into Khe Sanh?"

"Some of it."

"When I got there in 'sixty-seven, there was only one road in and out. Highway Nine all the way from Ca Lu. One lane, through some of the worst territory you can imagine. NVA everywhere. From midnight to noon the road went in, from noon to midnight it went out. They'd have one of us in a tanker truck, driving five thousand gallons of JP-4, sandbags on the floor, an M-16, and that's it. One man. I made that run about a dozen times. Saying every prayer I knew along the way."

"Maybe it helped."

"Maybe it did. But what I didn't find out until later was the philosophy behind it, the way it operated. Our guys were getting blown up all the time, mines, snipers, RPGs. There was no way to hold and control the jungle around the road. The logistics officers figured we were losing an average of three to five percent of everything that tried to get through. No matter what they did.

Three to five percent of the supplies lost, three to five percent of the men killed."

"That must have been tough."

"You know what solution they came up with?"

She shook her head.

"Add five percent more men, supplies, trucks. Make your losses sustainable. Get more trucks, more men out on that road so you can lose five percent without impacting the efficiency of the base. It made sense, unless you were one of those guys that didn't get through, or their families."

"Doesn't seem fair."

"Fair or not, it worked. You know what that's called?"

"What?"

"Management. Take it easy out there, Sara. Be safe."

She found herself out on CR-23 almost without realizing it, headed south, the window down. Cooler today, with a breeze blowing through the sugarcane. In the canal to her left, she saw a gator sunning itself on the bank, as they always did when the water temperature dropped. It was her first time out here since the shooting.

When she came over the rise, she saw the white cross ahead on the shoulder, at the top of the incline that led down to the swamp. *What the hell is that?*

She slowed, pulled over, heard gravel under the tires. She killed the engine and got out, slipping the handheld into her belt.

In the distance, she could see the hulk of the old Highfield sugar refinery, sun glinting off what was left of its windows. Beyond it, acres and acres of scrub pine, dead fields. To her left, sugarcane bent in the soft wind.

The cross was white Styrofoam, about a foot high. A spot had been cleared in the gravel, the spiked base driven into the dirt. A teddy bear was wired to its shaft, a handful of flowers in a small plastic vase in front of it. They moved gently in the breeze.

A wallet-sized photo had been thumbtacked to the center of the cross. A young black man in a cap and gown, gold-rimmed glasses. A posed shot, high school graduation. She thought about Derek Willis lying facedown in the wet grass, his clothes soaked through with blood, his eyes open.

She stood there for a while, alone by the side of the road, looking down at the cross, hearing nothing but the wind.

There was only one real motel in town, the Starlite, on Sawgrass Road. It had a fifties-era red neon sign that advertised FREE TV and LO RATES. A smaller sign over the office said AMERICAN-OWNED.

Sara parked the cruiser in the lot, left the engine on. There were half a dozen cars outside the adjoining coffee shop, a cab. If the woman was staying in town, she was here.

She considered going into the office, asking if a Simone James was registered. Then waiting out here for her to show up, however long it took, to get a better look at her.

After a while she got her cell out, called Billy's home number. It rang six times and the machine picked up. Lee-Anne's voice. Sara ended the call.

The lot at Tiger Tail's was nearly full, mostly pickups, at least two with Confederate flag bumper stickers. In the back window of one was a decal that read TERRORIST HUNTING PERMIT.

Billy's truck was parked alongside the fence. She pulled the Blazer in behind it. She'd gone home, showered, made dinner for her and Danny, waited for JoBeth to show up.

Crowded for a Tuesday night, eight o'clock and the after-work crowd still hanging in. Sara went in to a blare of smoke and noise, Johnny Cash's "I Still Miss Someone" on the jukebox, Billy at it again.

He and Lee-Anne were at the bar, their backs to the door.

*You surprised by that? Turn around, walk out. Smartest thing you could do.*

Althea waved from the bar. Billy turned, saw her. Lee-Anne turned then, too. Sara lifted her chin at them, went to the far end of the bar, found a spot. Althea brought her a pint of Guinness.

"Sam's here," she said.

"Where?"

"Over there." She gestured toward the back alcove. Elwood was at the pool table alone, stretched over the felt, sizing up a shot, cigarette hanging from his mouth. He was out of uniform, wearing jeans and a red Western shirt with pearl snaps.

"Want me to start a tab?" Althea said.

"No." Sara got bills from her pocket, put a five on the bar. "I'm not staying long."

She picked up the Guinness, walked back to the alcove. She heard the click of balls, the thump of the shot going in.

"Who's winning?" she said.

Elwood turned, squinted at her through smoke. "Hi, Sara." He tapped the cigarette into an ashtray on a shelf, picked up the bottle of Coors Light next to it.

"Surprised to see you here," she said.

"Old Luke lets me off the leash every once in a while. Figured I'd come by, grab a beer."

"Loose definition of beer."

He gave a short laugh. "I guess. Rack 'em up."

She put her Guinness on the shelf, got the rack from the wall peg. He squatted, fed quarters into the slot. The balls clacked, rolled out.

She set the rack, put the balls in, the one ball in the top position, eight ball in the center, lifted the rack away. He chalked his stick.

"Eight ball?" he said.

"Good enough. Calling shots?"

"Might as well."

She got a cue down from the rack, tested its weight, chose another, heavier one.

"Shoot for the break?" she said.

"No, you go ahead."

She chalked, placed the cue ball, leaned over the table, her weight equally distributed, knees slightly bent. She shot to the right of the one ball, hard and fast, the way her father had shown her. The balls flew apart. The fourteen ball spun, dropped into a corner pocket.

"Stripes," she said, walking around the table to the other side. The rim was marked with ancient cigarette burns. Elwood sipped beer, watched her. She picked her shot, leaned, eyed the setup, pointed the stick at a side pocket. She hit the nine off the eleven, watched it drop.

"Glad we're not betting on this," he said.

She missed her next shot, watched the twelve carom harmlessly off the rail.

Elwood put his cigarette down, blew smoke through his nose, hefted his stick, and circled the table. Sara looked back into the bar. Lee-Anne had her left arm linked in Billy's right, had pulled him close. He was listening to her, nodding. He looked over his shoulder at Sara. She met his eyes for a moment, looked away.

Elwood sank his shot, took another, missed. She looked back at the table and for a moment couldn't remember if she had stripes or solids. Elwood was watching her.

She eyed a combination on the eleven, shot and missed.

"You're distracted," he said.

She chalked up. "I guess."

He walked around the table, looking for his shot.

"Our friend's out a lot these days," he said. "He should be keeping a lower profile."

He sank the five ball.

"Is that what you're doing here?" she said.

"Keeping an eye on him?"

He stretched out for a shot, looked up at her, then back at the table, hammered the three ball into a corner pocket. "Maybe somebody needs to," he said.

She sipped Guinness, looked out to the bar. Billy and Lee-Anne were standing, ready to leave, arms still entwined.

Elwood missed his next shot. Sara looked away from them, back at the table.

"Your shot," he said.

She put the Guinness down, shot for the eleven again, missed. She heard the front door open and close.

"I can't remember the last time I saw you miss two shots in a row," he said.

"Can't seem to concentrate."

"No wonder on that." He bent, missed an easy shot on the four.

"Don't do that," she said.

"Do what?"

"You know what I mean."

He shrugged, got his beer.

She looked at him, then down at the table. She chalked up, leaned for the shot, used the ten ball to put the eleven in the side pocket. The cue ball came to rest midtable, gave her an easy setup with the fifteen in the far corner. She sank it hard, watched the cue roll back into position for another shot at the ten.

"That's more like it," he said.

She sank the ten, ran the table. The eight ball lingered near a corner pocket. She pointed the stick at the pocket, and he nodded. She chalked, bent, put it in.

"Like I said, glad we weren't betting."

"Good game, Sam."

"Go again?"

She shook her head. "No, I've got to be getting home."

She put the cue back on the rack. The pint of Guinness was still half full, but she was done with it. She carried it back to the bar to save Althea a trip, went out the front door. It shut behind her, muffling the music. She got her keys out, headed for the Blazer.

Billy's truck was still there. Light wash from a pole fell at an angle across the windshield. She could see him in the driver's seat, alone, head back, eyes closed, as if he were sleeping.

As she walked by, he opened his eyes, saw her. He said something she couldn't hear, and then Lee-Anne raised her head up from under the dash, looked out at her.

Sara felt the warmth rush to her face. Lee-Anne met her eyes, smiled. She pushed her braids away, turned and spoke to Billy, then powered her window down. Billy sat there, frozen, blinking.

Sara couldn't move. Lee-Anne looked out at her.

"You want to come over here and watch?" she said. "See how it's done?"

Sara turned away, walked to the Blazer, her face burning. Behind her, Lee-Anne laughed. Sara got behind the wheel, turned the key, ground the starter, had to switch the ignition off, try it again.

Lee-Anne looked back at her, then dipped her head again, disappeared from sight. Sara heard a low moan from the truck, one she knew well.

She backed out, turned the wheel, pulled fast out of the lot. She was a mile down the road before she realized she was speeding. She willed herself to slow down, her face still flush and hot. It was the tears that surprised her.

# EIGHT

When the knock came at the door, Morgan got the Beretta from the nightstand, looked through the peephole. C-Love and Mikey were outside.

"Come on, man," C-Love said. "It's freezing out here."

Morgan undid the lock and night latch, opened the door, the Beretta at his side. As they came in, he looked past them into the parking lot. The Suburban was parked in the shadows near a Dumpster.

"The twins out there?" he said. He shut the door, locked it.

"Yeah, why you ask?" C-Love said. He was carrying a black plastic grocery bag. Mikey walked around the room, poked the bathroom door open.

"What are you looking for?" Morgan said.

"Nothing."

"You bring what I asked?"

C-Love hefted the bag, dropped it on the bed.

"We need to talk about some shit," Mikey said. There was a table and chair under the front window. He pulled the chair out, straddled it.

"That boy you murked in the alley," he said. "That was Philly Joe from around the way."

"So?" He set the Beretta on the night-stand.

"His people gonna be looking for you."

Morgan went to the bed, opened the bag. Inside was a ziplock plastic bag filled with greenish-gold marijuana. C-Love stood near the door, watching him.

A plane came in low overhead. The lamp on the nightstand rattled.

"That's good shit," C-Love said. "Best hydro around right now."

Underneath, two brown plastic prescription bottles without labels. He twisted the top off one, saw the Vicodin inside.

"What you need that shit for, dawg?" Mikey said. "You never told me."

The tablets were five milligrams each. Morgan broke one in half, put it on his tongue. He dropped the other half back in the bottle, put the cap on. He went into the bathroom, palmed water, swallowed it.

"That shit will fuck you up," Mikey said.

Morgan drank more water, came out of the bathroom.

"You scarfing down those pills so quick," Mikey said, "you don't even see what else is in the bag."

Morgan looked. There was a black plastic bundle at the bottom, ends taped shut with duct tape. He drew it out, knew what it was. "This for my trouble?"

"That's an advance," Mikey said. "I need you to take that little trip for me. Shit I told you about."

"How much is in here?"

"Five Gs."

"Not much."

"For expenses, for now. Traveling money. Good timing, too, since Philly's boys looking for you. There's that thing with Rohan, too. Gonna be a while before all that shit quiets down."

"You talk to them?"

"That Trey Dog crew? Can't do that just now. They're screaming for blood, and they know you with me. I can get messages back and forth, with an intermediary. But I gotta watch my back on this, too."

Morgan sat on the edge of the bed. "Tell me about this trip."

"Told you some of it. Pipeline's been dry

since the Colombians went down. Even if they beat the case, they ain't gonna be up and running anytime soon, if ever. Now I got this RICO shit hanging over my head, and these lawyers, man, they keep wanting more."

"Go on."

"Word was some Haitians down in Florida had a good line on powder, shit coming in through the islands. They the new power down there now. Making mad money. We set up a meeting, place called Belle Glade. Curtis went down there." He nodded at C-Love. "It looked good. They had their shit together, steady source, but they don't know me well enough to want to do business. And those voodoo motherfuckers don't trust anyone didn't grow up poor and barefoot like them."

"So you sweetened the deal?" Morgan said.

"You know my cousin Leon? He in Rahway now, longtime, but he used to run those corners down near Baxter Terrace. His son Derek was wanting to get ahead, put some work in. Smart boy, too. Going to Rutgers, wanted to be a teacher or some shit. But he got a little one now, a baby mama, too. He needed cash, you know? He came to me, wanted me to help him out, bring him along a little. So I gave him a shot."

"You sent him down there?"

"Set him up good. Route, expenses, every damn thing. He had a cash advance for the first shipment, prove we were serious."

"How much money?"

Mikey twisted a thick gold ring on one finger. "A lot, man. More than I could afford."

"How much?"

"Three hundred fifty K. I threw in some iron, too; as a gift. Island boys love their guns."

"Why didn't you send the twins?"

"With their jackets? Some cop pull them over, think he hit the lottery. Derek was clean. No sheet on him."

"What happened?"

"Some shit I still ain't figured out. He got pulled over in some cracker town down there. They say he drew on a deputy, but that's bullshit. They capped his ass and took my money."

"You know this?"

"Much as I need to. I ain't known Derek to ever carry, but he might have been, I don't know. Might have got nervous, cash in the car, dealing with some niggas he didn't know. But shoot it out with a cop? Nah. He ain't got the stones."

"Maybe he got scared."

"Maybe he did. Maybe it happened exactly like they said. But ain't nobody said shit about the money yet. And it was in all the papers down there. They impounded the car, probably ripped the thing apart. If they found the money, some motherfucker took it."

"Or they're holding it and not telling anybody. Waiting to see who comes looking for it."

Mikey shook his head. "There ain't no DEA, no FBI involved in this. If there was, I'd have heard. This is a bunch of redneck Confederate-flag-flying small-town motherfuckers. Whether it was one motherfucker or two, or the whole goddamn town, fact remains. Somebody stole my money."

"Hard to believe you sent that boy down there on his own like that."

"Best way to do it. Down there, two niggas in a car get pulled over for sure. Cash was in a panel under the trunk. All he had to do was leave the car where we told him, then rent another, drive back. Didn't have to deal with them any more than that."

"So it went bad. Nothing you can do about it. Walk away."

"Can't take that kind of loss. Not now. Too much shit going on. I need that money or I need that powder so I can sell it and make that money back. Now I ain't getting any product out of those Haitians, because that money never got to them, and they not gonna believe me when I tell them what happened. Or care, even if they did. So I need that money."

Morgan got up. The Vicodin was kicking in, easing the tension in his stomach, taking the edge off the pain. He went to the window, bent the blinds, looked out. It was raining lightly, the parking lot shiny with it. The Suburban hadn't moved.

"If the cops do have that money," he said, "they're using it to build a case. No way you're going to get it back. And if someone stole it, they stole it. Either way, it's gone."

"If some nigga broke into my house and stole three hundred fifty K of my money, you think I'd let it go? Say, 'what the fuck, it's gone, forget about it'? Just because that shit happened in Florida doesn't mean it's any less fucked up. If I start letting people steal from me, I might as well pack this shit up right now. Or let some motherfucker put a bullet in my head, get it over with."

"I still say walk away."

"I can't, dawg. I need that money. I need you to go get it for me."

Morgan looked at him, then at C-Love.

"This shit can't stand," Mikey said. "I need that money. That's *my* money and I'm going to get it back, whatever I need to do. I don't have no choice."

"I do," Morgan said.

"You do. But you ain't even asked me the terms yet."

"Terms?"

"Three hundred and fifty K," Mikey said. "No way whoever took it could have spent it yet. All the shit in the news down there, they'd be laying low. So somebody dug a hole and buried it till things calm down. You find it, keep a third. You find the whole three fifty, you keep an even hundred twenty. That fair?"

*A hundred and twenty thousand,* Morgan thought. Combined with what was in the safe deposit, it might be enough for the treatment, maybe enough to get him started in another town. More money than he'd ever had at one time before. Might ever have again.

"Well?" Mikey said.

"I don't know anything about the South. D.C.'s the farthest I've ever been."

"You don't need to know shit about the South. Like I said, that's a backwater cracker town, man. They still burning crosses and fucking their sisters. I've already got someone looking into things down there."

"Who?"

"Derek's shorty. She went down there to bring the body back. She ain't too happy with the way things played out, but there it is. He took the chances. She don't want shit to do with me, but she's looking into things, seeing who's who, what they say happened, all that shit. Maybe she gets us some names, too."

"And then?"

"You go down there, straighten that shit out, get my money, and bring it back here. Take your cut. Then we clear."

"You make it sound easy."

"It ain't nothing you haven't seen before, dealt with. It's the same thieving bullshit, man. That's all it is."

Morgan scratched his elbow, looked at C-Love.

"You're the only one I can trust with this," Mikey said. "If you get down there and it don't work out, then it don't work out. I'll pay you for your time."

"How much?"

"Twenty K."

"I'll need to think on this."

"All right. But one other thing. If you do find the motherfucker that got my money?"

"Yeah?"

"You need to put him in the ground. Cop, sheriff, judge, mayor, whatever. I don't give a fuck. Put him in the ground."

The machinery clicked, hummed, and Morgan slid into darkness. The plastic table was cold through the thin hospital gown. Wraparound safety glasses blocked his view, but he could sense the walls of the tunnel closing in around him. A steady hum grew louder, then faded. The table buzzed, slid him farther into the tunnel, stopped. Then the hum again, rising and falling like something in a science fiction movie.

He tried to slow his breathing, fight the gathering fear. He counted his breaths as the table juddered, moved, and the hum rose again. Four more times and then the last hum faded and the table slid back out of the tunnel. He was slick with sweat.

"Take your time getting up," a voice said. "You might be a little dizzy."

He blinked as the glasses were drawn away. A black woman in flowered hospital scrubs stood beside the table.

"All done," she said. "How do you feel?"

He sat up. The room was dim, light coming through a window in the far wall. He could see two technicians behind the glass, neither of them looking at him.

"I'm fine," he said.

"You can get dressed now."

He went into the small anteroom, the tiles cold under his bare feet, pulled on his clothes. Soft music was being piped in, some white girl singing about rain on her wedding day.

When he was dressed, he went out to the main desk, stood at the counter. The woman in flowered scrubs was typing on a computer.

"You're all set, Mr. Morgan," she said. "Dr. Kinzler will get the results this afternoon."

"How do I pay?"

"We'll bill you," she said. She peered at the screen. "Are you still at this same address?" She gave the name of the hotel.

"I may be moving," he said.

"I'm sure we'll catch up to you," she said without looking up. "We always do."

Outside the hospital, he used his cell to call a cab. He hadn't wanted to drive the Monte Carlo around Newark in daylight. Around him, a half-dozen people, some in scrubs with no coats, smoked cigarettes, shuffled in the cold. None of them seemed to notice him.

■ ■ ■ ■

It was nine o'clock, and he was watching cable news with the sound low, stretched out on the motel bed, the Beretta beside him. On the nightstand, his cell began to buzz. He reached for it.

"Mr. Morgan? Dr. Kinzler."

Morgan sat up, used the remote to mute the TV.

"Sorry to call so late, but the MRI results got back quicker than I expected. I'm tied up here in the office anyway, so I thought I'd give you a call."

"What did you find?"

"I know Dr. Rosman probably explained to you how goblet cell manifests itself. It's a slow grower. If we diagnose early and get all the tumors out, we have a pretty high curability rate."

"What are you saying?"

"That pain you're having in the abdomen. The MRI shows a series of tumors in your small intestine. They're confined to that area, though, from what we can see. That's good."

On the TV, a woman anchor mouthed words, stock market prices crawling along the bottom of the screen.

"Mr. Morgan, are you there?"

"How many?"

"What?"

"Tumors."

"Maybe seven in all, from what I can see. They're small. I wouldn't say any are more than one centimeter in diameter, though we won't know for sure until we get them under a microscope. At that size, there's a good chance they haven't metastasized yet."

He laid a hand on his stomach, thought about what was there, beneath the skin, beneath the muscle. His body betraying him.

"What do we do?" he said.

"We go in there as soon as we can. Take them out, have a closer look. If we get them all and there's no immediate recurrence, you'll be in good shape. However, there's always the chance of undetected microscopic cells remaining, though they might not show up for a number of years. We'll keep you on a steady program of surveillance, testing."

"Then what?"

"If they occur again, we'll go to the chemo. But Mr. Morgan, all this is speculation until we get in there and have a look. Have you been having issues with diarrhea or difficulty breathing? A flushing of the skin maybe?"

"No."

"If you do, let me know. We need to move on this as soon as possible. Until I can examine the tumors, we can't decide the best route to go with treatment. I can't overestimate how important time is here."

Morgan heard a warning tone. The phone was nearly out of minutes.

"I need to leave town for a little while," he said. "Do some business. Couple, maybe three weeks."

"Can you postpone it?"

Morgan took a breath. "No."

"Then that puts us into mid-November, and, as I said, we don't want to hesitate too long here. There are other things that need to be handled as well. Pre-op testing, paperwork —"

"I know. Do what you need to get it started."

"Have you looked into any of the things I mentioned, as far as insurance is concerned?"

"No."

"You should. This could turn into a long and costly process."

Another tone, only a few seconds left.

"Set it up," Morgan said. "When I get back I'll call you, and we'll do this thing.

I'll have the money."

"Call my office as soon as you get back, Mr. Morgan. And I mean *that* day."

"I will," Morgan said, and then there was a final tone and the phone was silent.

# NINE

Sara was in the kitchen, drying the last of the dishes from dinner, when her cell trilled on the counter. She looked at the display. Billy's number.

It was a little after eleven, Danny asleep, JoBeth home. After leaving Tiger's, Sara had driven aimlessly, until the crying stopped, not wanting JoBeth to see her like that. She felt tired, drained.

The phone trilled again. She wiped her hands on a dish towel, picked it up. Thought about pushing the SILENCE button, setting it back down, ignoring it.

She hit SEND.

"Hey, Sara. I'm glad I got you."

She leaned back against the counter, closed her eyes.

"Sara? Are you there?"

"I'm here. What is it?"

"I'm really sorry about that. I don't know what to say."

"You don't have to say anything."

"It's Lee-Anne. Sometimes she's just . . . I don't know."

Something flared inside her. When she'd seen them in the truck, she'd felt only shame. Now came anger.

"Billy, I don't want to have this conversation."

"I embarrassed you, and I'm sorry about that. I shouldn't have let that happen."

"It's none of my business."

"I'm trying to apologize, Sara. Can you let me do that? Just this once?"

There was something in his tone, almost a pleading, and she felt herself soften. She shifted the phone to her other hand.

"I don't know what to say, Billy. I don't know what you want me to say either."

Silence on the line.

"Billy?"

"I used to be able to make you laugh," he said. "I loved that sound."

"Billy, please —"

"I'm sorry it all ended up like this."

She felt the sadness then, moving like slow fatigue through her body. *You are not going to cry. Not now.*

"I'm sorry too," she said.

"I'm getting you upset again. I didn't mean to."

"Billy, I've got too much going on in my life right now to deal with this. To deal with you. We make our choices, and we live with them. I'm living with mine. Why can't you do the same?"

"I'm trying," he said. Something seemed to break in his voice. "I'm trying my best, Sara."

"It's late. I have to go."

"I'm sorry for everything," he said.

"Good night, Billy," she said, but he was already gone.

At 2:00 A.M., she was still awake. She looked at the red numbers on the night-stand clock, pushed the covers aside. The central air was on, but it was still warm. She lay in the darkness, thought about Billy, remembered his hands on her.

*You ended it. It was your choice. And it was the right one.*

For months after she'd found out about Angie, she'd kept her distance from him. He'd made promises, pleaded with her, cried on the phone, but her humiliation had been too fresh, the hurt too deep. She'd see him at the SO or Tiger's, but always with others around. Later on, when her anger had come to seem pointless, irrelevant, there had been long nights when she'd wished he would call. He never had. Then Lee-Anne had come along.

She rolled onto her side, pulled the other pillow closer. It was cool against her skin. *You have to get up in four hours. You need to sleep.*

She closed her eyes, trying to will herself to sleep, knowing it was no use. Realized then she was damp. Her hand crept down to the waistband of her sweatpants, tugged at the drawstring. Her nipples were already hard, pushing against the thin T-shirt.

When the sweatpants were loose, she slid her hand in, found her wetness. She imagined Billy standing in the darkness, a silhouette against the window, then turning to her, coming closer. She could almost feel him there in the dark, smell his skin, hear the creak of the bed as he lay down, reached for her.

Then she heard Lee-Anne's laugh. Saw her face through the truck window, remembered the way she'd felt then.

She took her hand away, feeling foolish and alone.

She lay there for a while, the moment gone. Then she got out of bed, tightened the drawstring, went to the window, looked through the blinds. The Blazer sat alone in the driveway vapor light. Dew glistened on its hood. In the distance she could hear a freight train.

*Four hours.*

She got down on the floor, did slow push-ups, breathing in and out with each one. Her arms tightened, ached, but she kept her rhythm, not speeding up or slowing down. Watching the carpet rise toward her, then pushing it away.

When she reached twenty-five, she stopped, her arms locked straight, sweat on her forehead. She held that for a moment, then slumped onto her back, sucking in air. After a few seconds, she rolled to her feet, lightheaded, her breathing deep and steady. She crawled back into bed, pulled the pillow toward her, held it tight. Almost at once, she felt herself drifting. She went with it, let sleep take her.

Sara pulled the cruiser into the lot of the Starlite, saw the woman through the coffee shop window. She sat alone, most of the tables around her empty.

Eleven in the morning and the temperature already in the eighties. Sara shut the engine off, wondered what she was doing, why she'd driven out here.

When she went into the coffee shop, Shirley Osteen greeted her from behind the register.

"Hi, Sara. Anywhere you like."

Simone James was in a booth halfway down, her back to the door. Sara started toward her, aware of the noise she was making, the creak of leather, the static-y hum of the radio.

The woman didn't turn. She had a cup of tea in front of her, a plate with the remains of breakfast. Beside it was a folded copy of the *Sunbeam,* the county's weekly paper, and a cell phone.

"Miss James?"

The woman looked up at her. She was younger up close, her skin the color of lightly creamed coffee. Her hair was straight, pulled back with a green jade barrette that matched her eyes. She wore a sleeveless blue blouse, and on her right shoulder was a dark tattoo of two Greek letters. Sara didn't know what they meant.

"May I sit?"

The woman watched her for a moment, then nodded. Sara slid into the booth across from her.

Under the blouse, Simone James wore a diamond-studded heart on a thin gold chain. It was simple, yet beautiful. Sara didn't envy it, knew it would look out of place on her even if she could afford it, but on this woman it looked like it belonged, had always been there, always would.

"I'm sorry for your loss," Sara said.

The woman met her eyes. Sara felt awkward, her confidence slipping.

"Miss James —" she began.

"Why are you here?"

"I was passing by, saw you. My name is Deputy —"

"I know who you are."

Sara sat back. "Good," she said. "Then you know —"

"I know all about you. You and the man that killed Derek. I know you were there."

"I wasn't," Sara said. "Not when it happened." Then regretted it, the words feeling like a betrayal.

The woman slid the paper across to her.

"This just came out," she said. "You read that story in there?"

Sara shook her head. She had the paper delivered, but more often than not it went into the recycling unread.

"It says Derek was a 'suspected drug dealer.' Why would they say that?"

"Miss James —"

"Because he was black?"

"There were weapons in the car."

"But no drugs. So what makes him a suspected drug dealer?"

"Newspapers print what they want."

"No. Town like this, newspapers print what you police tell them. Am I right?"

"I wouldn't know."

Sara thought about getting up, leaving, but that would be a concession, a sign of weakness.

Simone James took a leather wallet from the seat alongside her, unsnapped it. She slipped a snapshot from a plastic sleeve, set it on the table between them. Derek Willis wearing a yellow T-shirt and an easy smile, holding a toddler against his chest, the child twisting to look at the camera. Trees in the background, people in shorts and T-shirts. Some sort of picnic.

"Go ahead. Pick it up, look at it."

"I can see it."

"Derek never hurt anyone in his life. He never carried a gun in his life, either. We met at college. Rutgers. Did you know that?"

"No."

"I graduated last year. Derek had a year to go for his degree. He wasn't no corner boy. There was no reason for you to shoot him down like that."

"Those weren't schoolbooks in that car."

"You don't listen, do you? Whatever was in that car, it wasn't his. Derek didn't have anything to do with guns. He was different from those boys he grew up with. He had a future."

Sara looked at the photo. The little boy's eyes. Derek Willis, young and alive, love for the child in his arms lighting up his face. She saw the gold ring in his right ear, the same ring she'd seen by the beam of the flashlight.

"I'm sorry," she said and meant it.

"He was a good man, and you people killed him like some animal."

Sara shifted in her seat. "I shouldn't have come here."

"Derek was twenty-two years old. Our baby is three now. Who's going to tell him what happened to his father? How am I ever going to explain that to him?"

"Where is he? Your son."

She replaced the photo in the wallet. "With my parents. I couldn't bring him down here. Not with what I have to do." Her voice almost broke then, lost some of its edge. "They won't give Derek back to me until they're done with him," she said. "With their 'investigation.' He's all alone down here. You people murdered him, then cut him up, put him on a slab somewhere. Now I can't take him home until they say I can."

There was wetness in her eyes. Sara looked away, out at the parking lot, the heat haze rising off the blacktop.

"I have a little boy, too," she said. "He's six."

"He have a daddy?"

"Yes."

"Where at?"

"I don't know. We're on our own."

"Why are you telling me this?"

"I'm not sure," Sara said. "I guess I just wanted you to know."

"Is he coming back? His daddy?"

"Maybe someday. I don't know."

"But he might. He might show up at your door tomorrow, to see you, see his son."

"He might."

"Derek won't. He told me he'd be gone a week, maybe a little longer, but he's not ever coming back."

The cell phone hummed on the table.

"I'm sorry I bothered you," Sara said and eased out of the booth. "And I'm sorry for what happened."

The phone hummed again.

"You may not be now," Simone James said, "but you will be."

"What's that mean?"

The woman looked at her, waiting, and Sara knew she was being dismissed. Her face felt hot.

"I'm sorry about what happened to your husband," she said. "That's all I came out here to tell you."

Sara held her eyes for a moment, then turned away, headed for the door. She nodded at Shirley, not trusting herself to speak, then pushed open the door and went out into the heat.

# TEN

When Sara ended her shift, Hammond's office was already dark, the door closed. Still in uniform, she drove out to his house on the far west side of the county, the road winding through shimmering cane fields. The air was filled with the harsh, sweet smell of a distant burn-off.

When she pulled up the driveway, he was out on the porch steps, tying flies, a tackle box open beside him. His cruiser and pickup were parked in the side yard. She pulled the Blazer up behind them, cut the engine.

He watched as she came across the lawn. He was out of uniform already, wore jeans and a blue workshirt.

"Figured I'd find you out here," she said. A wind chime on the porch sounded in the breeze.

"Knocked off early," he said. "Don't tell the taxpayers."

He set the fly in the box, stood, took a handkerchief from his back pocket, wiped his hands.

"Something wrong?" he said.

She shook her head.

"Then come on up. Get out of that heat."

He held the screen door for her. She went into the coolness of the hallway, a ceiling fan turning above.

"I made some sweet tea a little while ago," he said.

She followed him into the kitchen. Through the doorway into the living room, she could see a TV table set up in front of a recliner. The television was on, the sound turned down.

"I leave it on sometimes," he said. "Company, I guess."

He opened the refrigerator, took out a pitcher. "Glasses up there," he said.

There was a sideboard against the wall, a shelf holding white china with blue rims. On it were two framed photographs. One was a studio portrait of his daughter, Laura, a young woman with Asian features, long black hair. The other was of his wife, Lien-Thi, who'd died of cervical cancer the year before Sara joined the Sheriff's Office. In the photo, she stood at the railing of a cruise ship in a Hawaiian dress, wearing a lei. She looked slightly embarrassed and impossibly happy.

Sara got glasses down from the cabinet.

"Have a seat," he said.

He poured tea, set the pitcher on the table, sat across from her.

"You hear from Laura?" she said.

He shook his head. "She's got her own life. She doesn't like coming back here unless she has to. Too many bad memories."

"Sorry to hear that."

"Another year and she'll take the bar. I thought she might get out here for Thanksgiving, but she says she's got too much going on. She's seeing a fellow, too, and I wouldn't be surprised if they end up getting married."

"You must be proud of her."

"I got pretty lucky, is the way I look at it. The Good Lord watches over drunks and fools, I guess, especially if they're fathers. She didn't have an easy time of it, growing up here. Between my issues and her mother getting sick . . ."

"Sounds like you did a pretty good job of it anyway."

"I don't know. Maybe she got where she is in spite of, rather than because of. That would be my bet. Only reason I kept this house after Lin died was I thought Laura might want it someday. Doesn't seem too likely now, though."

Sara drank her tea. It tasted of honey and mint.

"I was up at the Starlite today," she said.

"Just for lunch, I hope."

"I saw that woman."

He sipped the tea.

"I went out there," she said. "Maybe I shouldn't have."

"And?"

"She thinks her husband was murdered. That Billy shot him without provocation."

He looked at his glass, swirled his tea. "She would, though, wouldn't she?"

"I guess."

"What else she say?"

"That I might not be sorry now about what happened, but I would be."

He frowned. "She say how — or why?"

"No."

"Did you take that as a threat?" he said.

"I wasn't sure how to take it."

"Well, she hasn't gotten a lawyer yet, far as I know. All her inquiries have been on her own. That bothers me, though, her bracing you like that."

"She didn't come to me. I went to her."

"Either way, it bothers me."

"She showed me a picture of her little boy.

He's three."

"I know. I saw it. What's on your mind, Sara? I mean exactly?"

She looked past him, out the kitchen window. The sun hung dark and red over the tree line.

"I met Elwood the other night," she said. "At Tiger's. Unusual to see him there."

"Sam likes a beer every once in a while."

"That's what he told me, but I got the impression he was keeping an eye on Billy."

"That might be the case."

"Then you don't buy his story? Our story?"

He put the glass down. "I told you I had some concerns," he said, "but not much more to go on than that."

"More than you let on, though."

He crossed his arms. "Nothing I'm about to say leaves this house. You know that, Sara, right?"

She nodded. *Here it comes.*

"Turns out Elwood had his own concerns, after the fact," he said. "He and Boone did the interview, but Boone wrote it, wanted to. Sam let him."

"And?"

"On paper, it all matches up. And everything that happened after you got there was strictly by the book, no worries there. Sam's

133

like a dog with a bone, though. Once he gets to chewing on something, he won't let it be."

"You told me it was a clean shoot, that's what they decided."

"There's not a single piece of evidence that says otherwise."

"Except Elwood's gut? And yours?"

"Sam came to me, told me he was ruling it in policy. Boone and the state attorney's office agreed. Then this Simone James set us both to thinking."

"You'd believe her over one of your own deputies?"

"Not at all. That's not what I'm saying."

"Maybe she didn't know what Willis was down here for."

"That's possible. Likely even. But let me make this clear, Sara. None of what Sam and I discussed is on paper, anywhere, and this department never has and never will be in the practice of airing its dirty laundry in public or to other agencies."

"Meaning what?"

"I signed off on the papers this morning. Flynn's free and clear. No charges of any kind. If there's a legal issue, a suit, that's something else, but as far as this department, this county, and the State of Florida are concerned, that shooting was one hundred percent justified."

"But you've asked Elwood to keep his eyes open."

"I wouldn't be doing my job if I didn't. And if it turns out there was more to that shooting than Flynn told us, I'm going to make sure he leaves this department with the kind of recommendation that'll keep him from getting another law enforcement job his entire life."

"You sound like you're already convinced something's wrong."

"Not at all," he said. "I just want you to know where we stand, and that all of this is in-house at the moment — you, me, and Sam Elwood. For the immediate future, that's how it's going to stay."

"I understand."

"How much do you know about Flynn's girlfriend?"

"Lee-Anne? Not much. She used to dance at the Sugar Shack out on Seventeen before they closed it down. That's how she and Billy met. He couldn't stay away from that place."

"I can see how you two wouldn't exactly be friends."

"She doesn't bother me."

"Brings into question his judgment, though, doesn't it?"

"It's none of my business anymore what he does," she said.

"Sam ran her through the computer, just for the hell of it. Turns out she had a couple minor arrests in Orlando back in the nineties — possession, shoplifting. Nothing much. But she did show up as a person of interest in a pending case. Seems that a couple days before the shooting, she went down to the West Palm area. That's where she was when it happened."

"I knew that. Billy told me."

"Sam's got a friend at the Palm Beach County SO, so he chased it down. She showed up during a surveillance down there. They ran the car tag, got her name."

"What kind of surveillance?"

"Narcotics case. Haitian gang. They're taking up where the Jamaicans left off, moving a lot of weed, coke. Got a big old house down there near Belle Glade, apparently all they do is party. Task force is working it — PBSO, FDLE, DEA. No arrests yet, but they're building a case."

"They sure it was her?"

"For the record, no, but the car was hers, St. Charles County plates and all. Sam got on the horn to Orlando PD. They found an old booking photo, faxed it down to West Palm."

"Sam's been busy."

"He has. An FDLE agent looked at the photo, was pretty sure it was her. White woman hanging out with all those gangstas couldn't help but catch their attention. She hasn't been back, though, as far as they know."

"What was she doing there?"

"Who knows? Just partying, maybe. She popped up on their radar, but they can't tie her to anything else. Maybe she just likes Haitians. You say Flynn knew she was down there?"

"Yes."

"He know who she was with, what she was doing?"

"He said she was with friends."

"I guess she was."

A breeze moved through the house, bringing with it the smell of cane smoke. The chimes on the front porch rang softly.

"I don't know," she said. "I don't know about any of this."

"You don't need to worry on it. But you asked, so I needed to tell you."

*But there's more you're not telling me. And you're not telling me because you're not sure you can trust me.*

"I should get going. Thanks for the tea."

They walked together back through the

house and onto the front porch.

"I appreciate what you're going through," he said, "and I know none of this makes it any easier. You've got enough on your hands as it is."

"I'll be okay."

"I know you will."

They walked toward the Blazer. To the west, the sun was slipping behind the trees in a dirty haze of smoke. She got her keys out.

"Been a while since I've been out here," she said. "I forgot how peaceful it is, quiet."

"Too quiet sometimes, with no one around. But it doesn't bother me that much. My life is pretty simple these days. I get up at six every morning, seven days a week, and I always have my Rule for Today."

"What's today's rule?"

"Don't drink. I can do anything else I want, but I can't drink. You know what the Rule for Tomorrow is?"

"What?"

"There is no Rule for Tomorrow. There's only today. And when I wake up tomorrow morning — if I wake up tomorrow morning — then the only thing I have to worry about is the Rule for Today."

"And that is?"

"Don't drink."

She opened the door, and he slapped her lightly on the elbow. She got behind the wheel and started the engine, and he stood there, watching, as she turned around and headed back down the driveway.

*Whatever you've done, Billy Boy, you've screwed us both.*

Her fingers tightened on the wheel as she drove. She missed the turnoff that would take her home, realized she was headed toward CR-23. She remembered what the woman had said. *You may not be now. But you will be.*

Heading south on 23, she topped the rise, saw the cross in the distance. Thought of what she should have said to her. *Why can't you just leave us alone? Why did you have to come down here and start all this? That boy's dead, he's never coming back, no matter what you do or who you hurt.*

When the cross loomed ahead, she braked hard, steered onto the shoulder. She got out of the Blazer, left the door open. The air reeked of burnt cane and, under it, the sulfur stench of swamp.

The plastic vase was overturned, the flowers gone, the photo sun-faded. The teddy bear tilted loosely, a single strand of wire holding it to the cross, its fur soiled by dust and rain.

She kicked at the cross, missed, lost her balance, almost fell. Then she reached down, pulled it from the ground. *Just leave us alone.*

She twisted, threw it. The cross sailed awkwardly through the air, landed in the wet grass, the bear a few feet away, face down. Where Willis's body had been.

She almost started down the slope to pick them up, throw them deeper into the swamp, out of sight forever. Caught herself, walked back to the Blazer.

She started the engine, U-turned off the shoulder, spraying gravel. A half mile later, she braked, pulled to the side of the empty road, and began to cry.

# Eleven

The Indian woman behind the counter didn't greet him, watched him as he made his way down the aisles. Basic foods, brands he'd never heard of, cans with faded labels. Stretches of dusty shelf with no product at all. Morgan remembered the A&P on West Market Street when he was a boy. A city block long, it had seemed. Endless rows of fluorescent lights, everything clean and bright. A store a boy could get lost in.

He picked up two overpriced quarts of motor oil, a handful of chocolate bars. There were no baskets, so he carried it all in the crook of his arm.

On a shelf near the counter, he saw a turn-rack of cassettes with sun-faded labels. A handwritten sign read 3 FOR $5. Stock left from the previous owners, he guessed. Nobody bought them anymore.

He scanned the titles, remembering what he'd left behind at the hotel. He chose a

Sam Cooke collection, O. V. Wright, the Impressions' greatest hits. The tape cases were covered with a thin film of dust. He found six he wanted, brought them to the counter.

The prepaid cells were on the wall behind the register, between hanging sheets of scratch-off lottery cards.

He pointed. "Two of those."

She scanned the items without a word. He pulled a roll of bills from the pocket of his leather, handed over three fifties. She frowned, unfolded them on the counter one by one, and passed a counterfeit detection pen over each. Then she opened the register, gave him his change, put everything in a single thin plastic bag.

He went out into the fading daylight, started across Elizabeth Avenue to where the Monte Carlo was parked. He'd taken the chance on driving. With the stops he had to make, a cab would be too much trouble. The bag dangled from his left hand, his right hand free. His coat was open, the Beretta in back. He put the bag in the trunk, got behind the wheel.

His next stop was three blocks away, a hardware store tucked between a fast-food chicken place and a shuttered shoe repair shop. He went up a flight of narrow stairs, through a glass door with an old-fashioned OPEN sign.

Otis was behind the counter, grinding a key. His hair had gone solid gray in the months since Morgan had last seen him. Reading glasses hung from a cord around his neck.

He saw Morgan, stopped what he was doing, the key machine winding down.

"My man," he said. "Long time."

"How you doing, Otis?"

"Day by day. Like everybody else."

Morgan took his outstretched hand in a soul shake.

"Took me a while, after you called," Otis said, "but I think I got everything you want."

"Solid."

Otis came from behind the counter, went to the door and worked the two dead bolts, flipped the sign to CLOSED. "Come on back," he said.

Morgan followed him behind the counter and into the rear of the store. Otis limped, a souvenir from an Aryan Brother who had stabbed him a half-dozen times with a bedspring shank. Two days later, Morgan had caught the Brother alone in a hallway off Five Wing and taken out both his eyes with a sharpened spoon.

It was overhot back here, smelled of metal,

oil, and dust. A radiator clanked. Morgan saw the double-barrel sawed-off that hung on pegs just above the inside of the door, within easy reach. Knew it was loaded.

Otis stopped at a tall shelf of plumbing supplies, put his glasses on, peered up at the boxes there. He took one down marked SHUT-OFF VALVES, set it on a worktable.

"There you go," he said.

Morgan opened it. Inside were five gray boxes of Winchester Super-X 9 mm shells, fifty rounds in each. Morgan thumbed one open, checked them.

"Early Christmas shopping?" Otis said.

"Something like that."

"You wanted to see something small, too, in a hand carry? I just got a couple new pieces in. Russian, but they're in good shape. I'd let them go cheap."

"Junk."

"Maybe, but they'll go quick. Corner boys love that shit. None of them can shoot worth a damn anyway."

"What else you have?"

Otis took a second box down, handed it over. Inside was a small black automatic wrapped in oilcloth.

"Walther PP," Otis said. "German police gun. Nine millimeter, like your Beretta."

Morgan took the gun out, ejected the

empty clip. The slide action was smooth, the gun recently oiled. No traces of rust. He pushed the clip back in.

"Light," he said.

"Get the job done."

"It's good."

"Got something else you might want to look at. Had it for a while, made me think of you."

He went to a shelf on the other side of the room, came back with a long, unmarked box, set it on the table. When he took the lid off, Morgan saw the short-barreled black-and-chrome Remington 12-gauge pump inside, resting on a bed of rags.

"Model 870," Otis said. "You used to keep one of them back when you worked for Poot O'Neal, didn't you? Around the time he got to warring with the Johnson brothers."

"Sometimes."

Morgan couldn't resist. He took the shotgun out, looked it over, feeling its familiar weight. He worked the pump, checked that the breach was empty, saw where the serial number had been filed off. After a moment, he shook his head, used a rag to wipe down where he'd touched it, put it back in the box.

"Not this time," he said. "I'm good."

He took the money roll out, peeled off

four hundreds.

"Too much," Otis said.

"It was a rush job."

"Twist my arm." He took the bills. "Let me give you something to put those in."

He went out front, came back with a cheap canvas gym bag, set it on the table.

"Been hearing some things about you," he said.

"Like what?"

"That you been going up against those boys from around the way. Took down a couple of their people."

"What else you hear?"

"That they looking for you. I see you in here buying all this, makes me wonder what you got in mind. There's a lot more of them than there are of you."

"My warring days are over."

"Don't look like that to me."

Morgan put the wrapped Walther and the ammunition boxes in the bag, zipped it shut.

"Let me ask you something," he said.

"What?"

"You ever sell to those Three Paw boys?"

"Sometimes. Why?"

"Doesn't matter."

Morgan hefted the bag, put out his hand. Otis took it. They clinched, released.

"We go back a long way," Otis said.

"Thirty years at least."

" 'Bout that."

"And you always one of my best customers. So don't take no chances you don't need to."

"I never do," Morgan said.

He put the gym bag in the trunk, headed back to the motel. On the way, he broke the seal on the Sam Cooke tape, pushed it into the player. "A Change Is Gonna Come" filled the car. It sounded like church. Like heaven. Like death.

"You all set?" Mikey asked.

"Good enough," Morgan said. They were in a parking garage downtown, Morgan leaning against the hood of the Monte Carlo, Mikey in the front passenger seat of the Suburban, the door open. Dante was at the wheel. C-Love stood a few feet away, smoking a cigarette, looking around.

"When you leaving?" Mikey asked.

"Tomorrow. Take me two, maybe three days to get down there."

"You could drive straight through, be there before you know it. I can get you some blow for the ride, keep you kicking."

Morgan shook his head. "I want my head clear when I get there. Couple things I need to know, though."

"What's that?"

"Willis's woman know what he was doing down there?"

"Maybe. Some of it, I'd think. Don't know how much he told her."

"She know how much money he was carrying?"

"Shit," Mikey said. "Even Derek didn't know that. No need. Package was in the car before he even picked it up. He was told to deliver the car, leave it. He didn't need to know shit else. Unless the boy was a total fool, he knew he had some cash in there, but not how much. He knew I wasn't paying him no four grand up front just to drop a car off."

"Four grand? That it?"

"For driving a car to Florida, leaving it somewhere? Yeah, four grand is fucking generous, yo. Plus he pull that off, come back and he'd have more work waiting for him. He knew all that. Knew the risk, too."

"His woman down there, asking questions, poking around. She finds out how much was in that car, don't you think she'll want a piece of it?"

"How she gonna find out? Who gonna tell her?"

"Don't know. With a little one and all, she

finds out, she might think she's entitled."

"Fuck that. She don't know, and no one's gonna tell her. You're gonna hook up with her down there, and she's gonna tell you everything she knows. I'll take care of her when she get back. I'll pay for the funeral, the flight and all that shit, too. She should be happy I'm doing that. Nigga got himself smoked, lost my money. She's lucky I'm not trying to take it out of her ass."

Morgan looked away. C-Love finished his cigarette, dropped it, twisted it out with his foot.

"I'll call you when I get down there," Morgan said. "Let you know what's going on, what the deal is."

"I'll send the twins down, you think you need them."

Morgan shook his head.

"Okay then," Mikey said. He put a hand out. Morgan touched knuckles with him. Dante started the engine as Mikey pulled the door shut.

C-Love got in the rear, closed the door. As the Suburban backed out of the spot, Mikey nodded at him through the tinted window. Morgan watched them drive away.

Cassandra moved naked across the room, lit the short, thick candles on the bureau top. Morgan watched her. He lay with a pillow behind his head, the sheet thrown aside. His skin felt warm, almost feverish.

When the four candles were burning, their incense filling the small room, she set the plastic lighter beside them. Soft light flickered on the wall, glinted off framed photos on the bureau.

"That okay, baby?" she said.

He nodded, and she slipped back into bed, curled against him, one hand on his chest, the wiry gray hairs there.

"I can feel your heart," she said.

He looked past her, through the open door into the other bedroom, could see the crib there, the night-light over it.

She traced his scars with her fingertips, lingered over the fresh one from his appendectomy.

"When are you coming back?" she said.

"Soon. I just have to take care of some things."

"You've been spoiling me. Sending me that money, and Aaron love those toys. But it feels like you haven't been by in a long time."

"Been busy."

He hadn't told her about being sick, wouldn't. He'd known her for three years now. She'd been nineteen when they met.

Her boyfriend worked for Mikey, had been killed in a police chase after making a delivery. The first time Morgan met her, he was bringing money from Mikey — five hundred dollars. It was all he would give her.

Morgan had added five hundred of his own, then come by to see her a week later with two hundred more, and then again the week after. That night she'd let him stay, and when he'd woken in the middle of the night, she was crying softly beside him. He hadn't known what to do, so he'd done nothing. After a while the tremors stopped and she slipped back into sleep. He'd come by once or twice a month ever since. Mikey didn't know about it. No one did.

He watched shadows play on the ceiling, then closed his eyes, felt her warmth against him, her softness. Wind rattled the room's single window.

He felt safe here, the only place now. Her breathing was slow and deep, and he found himself falling into rhythm with it, drifting into warm darkness.

He woke all at once, his eyes snapping open, muscles rigid. A draft from somewhere made the candles flutter. She murmured something against him but didn't wake. After a while, he disentangled from her, went to the window. He looked down on the empty street. A plastic bag scudded into the light from a streetlamp, then blew higher and out of sight.

He dressed without waking her. When he was done, he took two thousand dollars from his jacket, folded the bills, and slipped them under the jewelry box on the bureau. Then he leaned over and softly blew the candles out one by one.

He let himself out of the apartment, used his key to lock the door behind him.

He was on the road by noon. He took Route 78 to the Turnpike, headed south. He'd bought a map at a gas station, knew it was a straight run to Florida. I-95 all the way to Jacksonville, then west on 301.

He'd disassembled the Beretta and Walther, wrapped them in oiled rags, and stored them in the spaces below the rocker panels, along with the boxes of shells, the bag of marijuana, and the pills. He couldn't take a chance having them in the car if he were stopped.

The Monte Carlo's tank was full, the fluids topped off, and it was running smooth and strong, the heater on low, the Impressions coming through the speakers, "People Get Ready." It calmed him as he drove.

# TWELVE

It was ten thirty when she heard the knock at the door. She was stretched out on the couch in sweats and sneakers, reading a Jude Deveraux paperback, her hair tied up. The knock came again, soft.

She put down the book, went to the front window, and inched the blinds aside. Billy was on the steps, holding a pizza box in one hand, a plastic bag in the other.

She undid the chain and dead bolt, opened the door, looked at him through the screen.

"Hi," he said. "Hope I didn't wake you."

She brushed a loose strand of hair from her eyes. "What are you doing here?"

He raised the box. "Thought you might be hungry."

"Have you been drinking?"

"Not at all. Just wanted to come by, see you. That's all. Figured I'd bring a peace offering."

"I never eat this late. You know that."

"Then do you mind if I have a slice? I haven't had dinner yet."

She unlocked the screen door, pushed it open.

"Thanks," he said. She held the door for him as he came in.

"Danny's sleeping," she said.

"I'll be quiet. I tried not to knock too loud, but I was worried you wouldn't hear."

She closed the door behind him.

"Long time since I've been here," he said.

She took the pizza from him, went into the kitchen. He followed her. She put the box on the table.

"Paper plates on top of the refrigerator," she said.

He set the plastic bag on the floor, got two plates down, napkins and a salt shaker, set them on the table.

"I'm not eating," she said.

"In case you change your mind."

A piece of Danny's artwork was on the front of the refrigerator, held there by magnets. A colored pencil drawing on construction paper of a blocky police car, a figure with a smiling face behind the wheel. Next to it he'd written in oversized letters MOM.

Billy looked at it, smiled. "He's getting

154

pretty good," he said.

"He's growing up."

"Are you going to let him trick-or-treat this year?"

"I don't think so."

"You should. I mean, what's the harm?"

"Well, that would be for me to decide, wouldn't it?"

"You're right." He sat, opened the box, the smell of the pizza wafting up. He dragged a slice onto a plate.

"This is the only house on the block with no decorations," he said. "Couldn't help but notice."

"I didn't want to make him feel worse. Remind him of what he was missing, that he couldn't go out with the other kids."

"Makes sense, I guess. If you say so."

She sat across from him. "How'd you know I didn't have company?"

"Just a feeling. I'll leave if you want."

"Eat your pizza first."

He slid another slice onto a plate, edged it toward her. She ignored it.

"You have anything to drink?" he said.

"Some Bass in the refrigerator. Ice water, soda."

"I'll take a Bass, if that's okay. Want one?"

"Sure."

He got up, took two bottles from the

refrigerator, opened them.

"You want a glass?" he said.

She shook her head. He set the bottles on the table, sat down again. She could smell his cologne.

"Where'd you park?"

"On the street. Didn't want to leave my truck in the driveway, get your neighbors talking. I got sausage. Hope that's okay."

"You trying to make me fat?"

"No. You're in great shape."

"For my age?"

"You know what I mean." He salted a slice, folded it, and began to eat.

She'd felt irritation when she answered the door but found it fading now. It was good to have him back here, in the closeness of the kitchen, sitting across from her. It reminded her of a better time, back when she was naive enough to think they would someday be a family.

She sipped Bass. It was cold and sweet. He reached for the plastic bag.

"I saw this today," he said. "Thought Danny might like it."

He took out a square box with a painting of a tyrannosaurus on it.

"Plastic. The parts snap together. They've got a whole series."

He put it on the table. She looked at it.

"That's a lot of parts," she said.

"I know. I was worried about that. The box says ages eight and up, but he's a smart kid. I figured he could handle it. Think he'll like it?"

"He'll love it."

He ate in silence for a moment, wiped his mouth with a napkin, drank Bass.

She looked at the slice in front of her, pulled a piece of sausage off with her fingers, ate it.

"That was a bad scene last night," he said. "I'm sorry."

"You already apologized."

"I need you to know that, though, how I felt."

She nodded, didn't look up.

"If I could make it up to you, I would," he said.

She turned away, looked out into the hall.

"I've got a better idea," she said. "How about we just never mention it again?"

"Okay."

She pulled off another piece of sausage.

"Pizza's good, isn't it?" he said. "I got it from Sabatico's. Haven't had one in a long time. Last time I was there the old man asked me how you were. He must have seen the look on my face. He let it drop."

"This where you ask me to feel sorry for you?"

"No. I know better than that."

She pulled the slice toward her, tugged it into ragged halves. She dropped one on his plate, wiped her hands on a napkin.

"Table manners elegant as always," he said.

"Shut up and eat."

She folded her half, bit into it. It was still warm, the cheese thick, the crust thin and crunchy the way she liked. She finished it in three bites.

"That's more like it," he said.

"That's an extra thirty sit-ups tonight."

"You've got nothing to worry about."

"You think it's easy, staying in shape with all the junk food and bad coffee I consume on a normal shift? It's not. It's work."

"I know. You always were more motivated than everyone else around you. One of the things I admired most."

He opened the box, pulled another slice onto his plate.

"Got a knife?" he said. "We'll do it right."

"I'll pass." She got up. "Back in a minute."

She went down the hall, looked in Danny's room. He was sleeping, face to the wall, the night-light the only illumination in the room. She pulled the door almost shut, left it open a crack. The old clock in the kitchen began to bong softly. Eleven o' clock.

She went back into the kitchen, washed her hands in the sink. The slice was untouched in front of him.

"So where's Lee-Anne tonight?" she said.

"I don't know. Home, I guess."

She dried her hands on a dish towel, turned to him. "How come you're not there?"

He shrugged, rocking on the chair, all his weight on the back legs.

"Don't do that," she sat. "It's bad for the chair."

"Sorry. I forgot."

He sat forward, let the front legs touch down. "I'll clean up," he said. He put the uneaten slice back in the box, got up and gathered the paper plates and napkins, put them in the trash can beneath the sink.

She went into the living room, looked through the blinds. His truck was parked down the street in the shadow of a willow tree.

She heard water go on in the kitchen, then shut off, heard his footsteps. She didn't turn. She felt him come up behind her, smelled his cologne, let him slip his arms around her waist, pull her tight.

She closed her eyes. His face was buried

in her hair, his chin on her shoulder. She knew his eyes would be closed. She felt his arms around her, strong but gentle, put her hands over his, fingered the thick veins, the knobby knuckles. A worker's hands. A man's hands.

He kissed the back of her neck, and she felt goose bumps rise, tilted her head to give him better access. *What are you doing? Why are you letting this happen?*

She pushed back against him, felt his hardness through the jeans. His lips explored the side of her neck, the hollow behind her ear. She reached back, felt his thickness straining against the material, the shape of him. He sighed softly and his hands came up, cupped her breasts through her sweatshirt. She was braless and her nipples responded, hard to his touch.

He turned her and she let him, eyes still closed. His lips brushed hers and she looked at him then, into those slate gray eyes, the question there. She lifted her lips to his in answer. He kissed her hard and she let his tongue into her mouth, felt his hands slide down her back, cup her buttocks. She closed her eyes as they kissed, let him guide her away from the window.

The backs of her legs were against the couch when he broke off the kiss, looked at her. She didn't turn away. His hands began to work at the drawstring of her sweatpants. She helped him, felt the pants sag around her hips. Then she was sitting on the couch and he was kneeling on the carpet, tugging the pants down her legs, exposing the gray Jockey panties she wore beneath. He slipped her right sneaker off, freed the pants leg. She lifted her foot to help him.

He kissed the inside of her bare calf, flicked his tongue behind her knee. She was wet and ready, knew he could tell. He kissed his way higher, then stopped and looked at her, cocked an eyebrow. She nodded and he reached up, caught the elastic of her panties and pulled in opposite directions. They tore almost soundlessly, and she felt the cool air against her wetness.

She put her hands on the back of his head, her fingers in his soft hair, and closed her eyes.

They lay in darkness, the central air whispering around them. He was propped up on two pillows, his left arm curled around her shoulders. She was looking at the ceiling.

"Hey," he said. "You all right?"

She eased out from under his arm. He watched as she got up and took her robe from the back of the door. She pulled it on, pushed her hair free of the collar, tied the belt, felt his eyes on her.

"Be right back," she said. She went out into the hall, listening. Danny's door was as she'd left it. She stepped closer, paused, could hear his breathing.

She went into the bathroom, closed the door, and turned on the light. She looked at herself in the mirror. *Why did you let that happen? Are you so lonely and horny that you forgot everything you know? Everything you learned the hard way?*

She sat and urinated, then washed her hands and face in the sink. She could smell the musk of sex on her body. She flipped the light off, went back to the bedroom, pushing the door shut against the resistance of the carpet.

He moved aside to give her room. She lay beside him with her robe on, felt his arm curl around her, pull her close.

"Been a while for you, hadn't it?" he said.

"Why do you say that?"

"I can just tell, that's all." He kissed the top of her head.

She laid her head on his chest, could feel the beating of his heart through muscle and skin.

"You want another beer?" he said. "Some water?"

She shook her head, put a hand on his stomach, felt the muscles there.

"I was surprised to see you the other night," he said. "At Tiger's."

"I saw your truck, figured I'd go in for a drink, say hello. I should have known better."

"I saw you talking to Elwood."

"Yeah, he wanted to shoot pool."

"That all?"

"What do you mean?"

"That all he wanted?"

She lifted her head from his chest, looked up at him.

"Yes," she said. "And that's what we did."

He stroked her hair.

"Hammond talk to you again?" he said.

"About what? He talks to me almost every day."

"About me."

"Nothing I haven't already told you," she said and felt guilty for the lie. "Do we have to discuss this now?"

"Just wondering." He rubbed her back through the robe. "Sometimes it feels like they're telling me one thing but thinking another."

"Who?"

"The sheriff. Elwood. You."

His hand slid down to the belt knot, played with it, drew on it until it was loose.

"I just don't want to get blindsided by anything," he said. She felt his warm hand on her bare stomach. It crept up, cupped her left breast. His thumb found her nipple, and it grew hard under his touch.

"If there was something else going on," he said. "If they were trying to nail me to the wall, and you knew about it, you'd tell me, right?"

"Is that why you're here?"

"No, of course not." His hand slid to her other breast. "I came here to see you."

She caught his hand, took it out of her robe.

"What's wrong?" he said.

She sat up, pulled the robe tight, knotted the belt.

"I'm sorry," he said. He touched her hair. "Don't get up."

"You need to get dressed," she said. Her feet found the floor.

"Come on. Don't be like that."

She got up, went to the window, looked out. It was raining, drops spotting the glass. Low thunder in the distance.

"Sara," he said.

She didn't turn.

"I shot that boy because he drew down on me. You know that. You were there."

She didn't respond.

"He was a bad guy, Sara. I'm lucky he didn't nail me first. It could have been me laying in that ditch."

"That sounds practiced," she said without turning.

"Sara, you know the way I feel about you. And I know the way you feel about me."

"Do you?"

"I used to, at least." She heard him get out of bed, his footsteps on the carpet. The rain was picking up, blowing against the window.

She felt him behind her. He pushed her hair aside, kissed her neck.

"Get dressed, Billy," she said.

He drew his lips away. "We were always good together, Sara. We could be that way again."

She turned, met his eyes. He was watching her, waiting.

"Hey," he said softly. "There's no reason to cry." He reached as if to brush her tears away. She stopped his hand an inch from her face.

"Please. Go."

He took his hand away.

"So that's the way we are," he said.

She didn't answer.

He went back to the bed, found his jeans and T-shirt on the floor.

"Thanks for your support," he said.

He pulled the jeans on, sat on the edge of the bed, reached for his boots. She looked back out the window.

He was taking his time, waiting for her to tell him to stop, not leave. Eventually, she heard him open the bedroom door and go out.

She followed him into the hall. He had the front door open, was looking out through the screen at the rain. She stopped in the hallway, leaned against the wall. He heard her, turned. She didn't look away, pulled the robe tighter.

"Okay," he said. "Then I guess that's the way it is."

He opened the screen, went out into the rain.

She went to the door, watched him sprint to his truck. When he reached it, he turned and looked back at her, sheets of rain moving down the street. After a moment, he opened the truck door, climbed up. She heard the engine start, saw his headlights go on.

*You're gone now, Billy. You're someone else. You're out of my reach. Maybe you always were.*

She watched him pull away. Then she shut the door and locked it.

# THIRTEEN

He made Virginia the first day, keeping his speed under seventy, though the Monte Carlo's big V8 wanted to do more. Other cars passed him in a blur.

He didn't stop for food, ate two of the chocolate bars instead.

When his eyes grew tired, the white line double, he found a motel off 95. The fat white man at the desk wanted identification. Morgan turned away, was leaving the lobby when the man called him back. When Morgan handed him seventy in cash, the man counted it twice.

In the room, Morgan spread the map on the bed and traced his route. He'd try to make Savannah tomorrow night, would drive as late as it took. Then into Florida the next morning.

His cell buzzed on the bed. He picked it up, saw it was C-Love's number.

"Yeah."

"Take this down," C-Love said.

"Hold on."

He went to the writing desk, got a sheet of motel stationery, a pen. "Go ahead."

"Where you at?"

"Place called Emporia."

"Where's that?"

"Virginia."

C-Love read off a ten-digit number. "Woman's name is Simone. She knows you're on the way. Hit her on that number when you get down there. She says she got some information for you."

"Anything I should tell her?"

"You don't need to tell her shit. Just find out what she got, take it from there. They released the body, so she getting ready to fly back. After you hook up with her, call me. Big Man'll wanna talk to you."

"After I hear what she says, I'll handle it my way, whatever I think is best. He knows that, right?"

"He knows. He just want to talk, see what your sitch is. See if you need some help."

"No help," Morgan said.

"Might change your mind when you get down there. Can't never tell how that shit's gonna play out."

"I'll call after I talk to her. Tell him that."

"I'll do that. You stay in touch, bro."

Morgan pushed END. He was feeling the miles, the ache in his back and hips.

He checked the lock on the door, set the chain. He felt vulnerable without the Beretta. He turned the TV on, the sound low, just to have another presence in the room. He folded the map, switched the lamp off, lay on the bed fully clothed, the TV light flickering on the walls. In a few minutes, he was asleep.

Crossing into Georgia, Morgan had the windows open, Bunny Sigler on the tape deck. Warm air blew through the car. Forest on both sides of the highway, green and thick. Then suddenly, on his left, a wide river running parallel to the road, the sun sparkling on its surface. After a few miles, the river turned, winding back through the forest like some primeval scene, a painting from a book.

He'd bought a pair of sunglasses at a Stuckey's in South Carolina and put them on now against the glare. He wore a gray pullover, sleeves pushed up, the leather coat folded on the backseat. The sun and breeze felt good. He hadn't taken a Vicodin that morning, hadn't needed it. He felt awake, alert, the highway unfolding in front of him, the air sweet. Newark felt like another world, another time.

He drove past billboards for pecan logs, fireworks. Past Waffle House and gas station signs mounted on high poles visible from the elevated roadway. Every few miles, he passed pieces of torn-up truck tires on the shoulder. He'd push as far into Georgia as he could, until the fatigue was too much, then stop for the night.

Tomorrow he'd cross into Florida, head west on 301, the route that would take him around Gainesville, then south again. I-75 part of the way, then local roads past Lakeland, deep into the heart of the state. He'd marked Hopedale on the map, had picked a town named Arcadia to stay in. It was in a different county, an hour northwest. Close enough to get in and out easily, far enough away that his presence wouldn't be known.

He turned the volume up. Bunny telling his woman he'd be home soon. A phone call from a bus station. Only a few more hours to go.

The trees dropped away on both sides, gave way to rows of white-tipped plants stretching forever, like a carpet of snow. Cotton fields, he realized. He drove on.

He crossed the border a little before noon and turned off I-95 onto 301, the map open on the seat beside him. For most of the ride, Florida had seemed like more Georgia, but now the terrain began to change. He passed swamps and canals, thick trees with hanging moss. Barns with tin-patched roofs, chickens in the yards.

He stopped for lunch outside Ocala, a fast food drive-through, and ate half a hamburger before his stomach rebelled. He sipped Coke to settle it, got back on the road. Soon he began to see signs for Lakeland. He found it on the map, traced the roads that would take him southeast.

Near Arcadia, he passed a row of unpainted shotgun shacks hard by the roadside. In front of one of them, two black children played in the dirt. They watched as he drove by.

Twenty minutes later, he found what he wanted. The motel was set back from the highway. It was a sixties-style motor court, U-shaped with semidetached cottages, all gray wood and clanking air conditioners. Only four other cars in the lot. The pool was empty and cracked.

The old black man behind the bulletproof glass in the office had no problem taking Morgan's cash. No maid service. Washer and dryer in back, quarters only. Ice machine free. Morgan paid for four nights in advance.

He pulled the Monte Carlo around back, out of sight of the access road. Trees back here, a narrow creek running through, and everywhere the rotten egg smell of nearby swamp.

The key was on a diamond-shaped piece of plastic. He let himself into the small room — a single bed, bureau, nightstand, desk, television, no phone. A jalousie door with roll-up shade. He turned the air conditioner on. It thumped and shook but eventually blew a stream of cool air into the room.

His pullover was soaked through with sweat. He peeled it off and tossed it on the bed. He pulled the heavy curtains shut, found they didn't meet. A band of sunlight still blazed through.

He touched his toes, held the position to let the tension in his back ease. It was good to be off the road. It had taken more out of him than he'd expected. He got his cell out, looked at it, then put it on the nightstand. He'd rest a while, then make the call.

He stretched out on the bed, closed his eyes, felt the miles start to fall away from him. He slept.

He was lying on the bed, fully dressed, when the tap came at the door. He looked at his watch. It was a little past nine.

He got up, edged the door shade aside. A woman stood in the yellow glare of the outside light. An oversized purse hung from her shoulder.

He opened the door. A cab that said SAINT CHARLES TAXI on its side waited in the lot, the white driver watching them.

"You need to pay him," the woman said.

"How much?"

"Fifty."

He got his wallet from the bureau, took out two twenties and a ten, gave them to her.

"You do it," he said. "Tell him to wait around, but not out there. Tell him to go somewhere, drive around, come back in twenty minutes. You won't be long."

"What if he doesn't want to wait?"

"Then he drives all the way back down there with an empty cab and no fare. Or he stays, makes another fifty dollars and a twenty tip. Tell him. He'll wait."

She went back out. Morgan switched off all the lights except the one on the nightstand. He heard the cab pull away. When she came back into the room, she shut the door behind her. He caught her purse strap, turned her, and had it off her arm before she realized it.

"Man, what the —"

He opened it. Cosmetics, wallet, cell phone, a thick white legal envelope. He took the envelope out, tossed it on the bed, shook the purse, saw there was nothing else in it. He handed it back to her.

"Your ass is paranoid," she said.

He went to the door, locked it. "Anyone follow you here?"

"No. I kept looking. I never saw anyone."

He pointed to the bed. She went over, sat on the edge, set her purse on the floor. He pulled the desk chair out and sat down, knowing he was in shadow. The way he wanted it.

She was younger than he expected. When he looked at her, he thought about Cassandra, felt something tug inside him. The woman wore her hair straight and back, designer jeans, a soft green man's shirt. He could sense her uncertainty, the fear she was hiding. Wondering if she should have come out here, what would happen next.

She looked at the door, then back at him.

"You talk to Mikey?" she said. "You know who I am?"

He nodded, pointed at the envelope. "What's that?"

"Police reports. Coroner's report, too. And two newspaper stories I cut out. The names are all in there. I found their addresses, too. The man who shot Derek is named Flynn. He had a woman cover for him, named Cross. They're the ones that killed him."

"You sure about that? About the woman?"

"She was with him."

She held the envelope out. He took it, put it on the desk.

"I'm leaving tomorrow," she said. "I'm taking Derek home."

"Good."

"What are you going to do?"

"About what?"

"Mikey said you'd take care of this. Take care of the people that hurt Derek. What happened to him wasn't right. He didn't deserve that."

*Mikey don't give a shit about Derek,* Morgan thought. *If you think he does, you're as big a fool as that boy was.*

Pain in his stomach then, the first time in days. He grimaced.

"You all right?" she said.

"What else you find out?"

"They said the case is closed. No charges."

"What about the car?"

"They impounded it. They're keeping it, I guess."

"They find anything else in it?"

"Like what?"

"Anything."

"Not that they told me. And there's nothing in those reports."

He got up, walked past her into the bathroom, took the Vicodin bottle out of his overnight bag. He shook out a half tablet, filled a plastic glass with water from the sink, washed it down. He could feel her watching him.

"Mikey give you anything for me?" she said.

"Like what?"

"Money."

He went back out, shook his head.

"He owes me for what happened," she said.

"You need to take that up with him."

He went to the window and pushed the curtains aside to look out. Insects fluttered around the outside light.

"Mikey tell you how much he paid Derek to come down here?" she said. "Four thousand dollars. That what his life was worth?"

He let the curtains fall closed.

"It's not fair," she said. He looked at her, saw water in her eyes. She blinked it away.

"He needed that money for us," she said. "For his little boy. That's the only reason he came down here. If he hadn't, he'd still be alive."

"You need some cash? I could give you a hundred or so."

He saw the anger then, pushing away the fear. Liking it, the strength there.

"A hundred?" she said.

"I can maybe go two."

"You're all the same, aren't you? You and Mikey and C-Love, all of them. You don't care what happens to anyone else, do you? It's all about the money."

"What did you think it was about?"

"We're owed," she said. "*I'm* owed. And my little boy. For Derek, for what happened to him down here."

*This woman is trouble,* Morgan thought. *Trouble for Mikey, trouble for C-Love. Once she walked out that door, though, not his trouble anymore.*

"Like I said, you need to get with Mikey on that."

"I will."

She stood, picked up the purse. "I'll wait outside. I don't like the smell in here." She started for the door.

"One thing you need to be careful of," he said. "When you get back up there."

"What?"

"Mikey don't pay his debts if there's a

cheaper way to solve the problem. You feel me?"

He got his wallet, took out three fifties, then, after a moment, three more, held them out. She looked at the bills.

"For the ride home," he said.

He kept them out there. She took them, then unlocked the door, went out, and shut it behind her.

He opened the envelope, took the papers out, got the reading glasses from his bag.

Copied reports, twelve pages altogether. One was from the coroner's office, had the generic outline of a body, front and back views, Xs marking entrance and exit wounds. Newspaper clippings and a plain sheet of white paper. On it, she'd written two names and addresses in a small, precise feminine hand.

He saw headlights, went to the window, and parted the curtains. The cab was there. She got in, looked back at the room, at him. Then the driver turned around and headed back the way he'd come.

He lay in the dark until one thirty, then went out to the car. The night was filled with the sound of crickets, the ragged hum of air conditioners, a muffled TV from one of the rooms.

He popped the trunk, got the bag Otis had given him, a screwdriver from the toolbox, the gun cleaning kit he'd bought at a sportsmen's shop in North Carolina. Then he opened the passenger side door, sat on the blacktop, and worked by the glow of the courtesy light.

When he was done, he replaced the rocker panels, locked the doors, carried the bag inside. At the desk, he cleaned and oiled the Beretta, then reassembled it. He spilled a box of 9mm shells out on the blotter, brass glinting in the light. He thumbed fifteen rounds into the clip, pushed it into the grip until it seated. He chambered a shell, decocked the gun, engaged the safety.

He did the same with the Walther, the gun only slightly heavier when it was loaded. When he was done, he took out the bag of reefer, got the pack of rolling papers from his overnight. The pain in his stomach was back, low and burning. He sat on the bed, lit the joint, sucked in smoke and held it, thought about the three hundred and fifty thousand.

Mikey's money, but he'd be inside before long, one way or another. Morgan knew if he brought it all back, Mikey would find a way to cheat him on the cut. Or just give him up to the Trey Dogs to make peace, keep it all himself.

With the three fifty and what he had stashed in Newark, Morgan could start again in another city, another state, bring Cassandra and the boy with him. He could find a doctor there, begin the treatments. If Mikey or C-Love or the twins came looking, he could deal with that, too, protect what was his. What he'd earned.

He put the Beretta in his overnight, left it unzipped, easy to get at. The Walther went under a pillow. He lay back on the bed, drew on the joint, let the smoke relax him. The pain in his stomach began to ease. He closed his eyes and listened to the night.

# FOURTEEN

After she clocked in, Sara went to the storeroom that held the SO's single general-use computer. She signed on, typed quickly, sat back and waited, hearing voices in the corridor, a toilet flushing down the hall.

When the report came up, she scanned it, hit PRINT. Behind her, the printer chattered. She looked toward the half-closed door, hoping no one would come in, ask what she was doing.

The printer spit pages, went silent. She closed the file and signed off. She gathered the pages from the printer, went out into the hall, and closed the door behind her.

One call this morning, a lawn mower stolen from a shed in Libertyville, and since then the radio had been mercifully quiet. At ten thirty, she parked the cruiser on a dirt road that led down to the river, lowered the window, shut the engine off. The drone of cicadas filled the silence it left.

She had a dull headache from the sleep she'd missed the night before. She had lain awake after Billy left, listening to the rain, wondering why she had let him back into her house, her bed. Not knowing the answer.

She read the report again. Little in it she didn't already know. Appended were Billy's statement, her statement, the medical examiner's report, and an inventory of everything found in the car and on Willis's body.

The wind shifted, moved the trees, brought the smell of the river. She looked through the inventory again. The recovered guns were listed by make and caliber: Ingram MAC-10 machine gun; Smith and Wesson Model 5906 semiautomatic; Heckler and Koch P7. All high-end weapons, with ammunition for each. Willis's gun was listed as a Taurus Model 85, .38 caliber, rubber grips, serial number burned off. She paged forward to the lab report. The only prints on the weapon belonged to Willis, full finger and thumb impressions. A 100 percent match.

She remembered the Taurus lying there in the wet grass, inches from his hand. The bluing had been nicked and scratched. With those better, flashier weapons in the trunk, why was he carrying that? She looked back at the inventory of ammunition. Six boxes of 9 mm shells. Nothing in .38 caliber. The Taurus didn't fit.

She left the papers on the seat, got out, and walked down the dirt track to the river. It was running low and muddy, wind feathering the surface. There was a clearing here, a collapsed dock, pilings protruding from the water. She realized then where she was. As a teenager, she'd parked here with Roy in his Firebird. Senior year of high school, before she'd gone off to college up north, thinking she was leaving Hopedale for good. *You'll be back,* he'd told her. He'd been right.

She sat on a flat rock, looked out at the river. On the opposite bank, dark trees rose like a hanging wave. A dragonfly flitted over the surface of the water, drifted on.

She picked up a stone, tossed it, watched the ripples spread.

*That's what life is. You make one decision, take one action, and it affects everything. It spreads out across your present, into your future. And it never stops.*

Life had seemed full of choices back then, opportunities. As she got older, door after door had shut. Now here she was, forty in sight, alone except for Danny.

*What decision are you making now?*

Had Elwood and the sheriff wondered about the Taurus, too? If not, with the investigation closed, Billy free and clear, what would be the point of bringing it up to them? What would that say about her?

She stood, dusted off her pants, and walked back to the cruiser, feeling totally and irrevocably alone.

When she got home, Danny was at the kitchen table, the Tyrannosaurus half assembled. She'd left it for him with a note, hadn't told him where it came from.

"Hey, little guy." She touched his hair. "How you making out?"

"Almost finished."

"You feed the rabbits?"

"Yup."

She got a bottle of water from the refrigerator, twisted off the top. She could hear the rumble of the dryer in the basement, JoBeth doing laundry.

There was a note on the refrigerator, held there by a parrot magnet. JoBeth's handwriting. *Dr. Winters called. 4:45.*

*Shit.* She looked at her watch. Five thirty. Still a chance to catch him if he was working late.

"When did you have pizza?" Danny said.

She realized then she'd left the box in the

refrigerator.

"Last night. I got hungry after you went to bed. We'll have the rest for dinner, okay?"

"It's cold."

"That's what microwaves are for, kiddo."

She got her cell out, went to her bedroom, speed-dialed the doctor's office. On the fourth ring, he picked up.

"Sara Cross," she said. "Returning your call. Sorry, I just got the message." She closed the door behind her.

"Hi, Sara. It's okay, I'm in the office trying to get my desk cleared anyway. Danny's lab results from last week came in, and I wanted you to know about them."

She swallowed, felt tightness in her stomach, tasted sourness. "Go on."

"As you know, one more treatment and we'll be reaching the end of the induction therapy. The new lab work shows we're on the right track as far as his T-cell count is concerned. I don't think I'm going too far to say we could be looking at a near-total remission by the end of the therapy."

She sat on the bed, closed her eyes. "But?" she said.

"We're not out of the woods yet. You know some of this already, but a patient like Danny diagnosed with ALL may have a hundred billion leukemia cells. When it's

186

successful — and in his case it looks like it is — induction therapy destroys at least ninety-nine percent of them. At that point we say the patient is in remission. However, that could still leave as many as a hundred million leukemia cells in the body. So we have to go after those aggressively. If not, they can grow and multiply later on and lead to a relapse."

"What are you saying?"

"That I think we should go ahead with what we talked about last time."

"More chemo."

"We call it consolidation therapy. It reduces and hopefully kills off the remaining cells. As I said, it takes about four to six months."

*Six more months.*

"Sara, you there?"

"I'm here."

"Consolidation therapy can be intense, especially at Danny's age, but I think it's the only way to go. We'll decide on the drugs and doses later. It won't be easy, but I think we have a good shot at whipping this."

"When do we start?"

"I have Danny's last induction session scheduled for two weeks from today. We'll see how that goes, what our test readings are, then come up with a plan for the consolidation stage."

"Okay."

"This is progress, Sara. Trust me. This far into the treatment, Danny's doing pretty well. The induction therapy, if it takes, leads to remission in about ninety-five percent of the children we treat. The consolidation therapy puts that figure even higher. So far, in Danny's case, it looks like it's taking extraordinarily well."

She went to the door, opened it, looked down the hall. She could see Danny at the kitchen table, his back to her.

"I don't mean to downplay the effects. The next few months will be rough. He'll have some of the same reactions to the chemo as he's had before, but hopefully not as pronounced or severe. We can talk more in two weeks, after his session, how's that sound?"

"All right."

"We'll see how he's feeling and take it from there."

She thanked him, ended the call. When she went back into the kitchen, Danny was sitting forward, elbows on the table, looking down at the last unassembled pieces. The dinosaur was no further along.

"Was that Dr. Jack?" he said.

"It was."

"Is that why you went to your room?"

"Just wanted a little privacy, that's all."

"Am I still sick?"

She looked at the back of his head, the patchwork of missing hair. She put her hands on his shoulders, squeezed gently, felt his warmth.

"Not for long, sweetie. Dr. Jack says you're going to be better soon."

He picked up a piece, placed it against another. They didn't fit. He put them back down.

"How soon?" he said.

*He's not letting you off the hook. He never does.*

"Soon."

He fit two pieces together, clicked them into place. The tail and back legs, the dinosaur almost done.

"Hey," she said. "I've got a better idea."

"What do you mean?"

"Better than leftover pizza. How about we hit the park before it gets dark, then get some burgers at Dairy Queen?"

"Can we?"

"If we leave now, sure. I just need to get changed. Are you ready?"

He snapped the final piece into place.

"All done," he said.

"Good job."

"It wasn't that hard."

"It would be for me."

"No, it wouldn't," he said. "You can fix anything."

The sun was sinking when they got to the municipal park, the carousel lights already flashing. Tinny calliope music, the smell of cotton candy and hot dogs from the push-carts. It was cooler now, and she'd made Danny put on a jacket before they left the house.

There were only a half-dozen kids on the carousel, all younger than him. For most of the town, the novelty of it had worn off in the year it had been here, but it wasn't until the past summer that she'd let Danny ride. "You baby him too much," Billy had said once, "You can't protect him from everything." She'd known he was right, but he didn't know what it was like to lie there at night, the house silent, imagining life without Danny. A life alone.

She bought tickets, helped him onto one of the horses, rode a circuit with him, and then stepped off, joining the other adults standing nearby. He waved at her as he went around, his other hand clutching the pole, his smile huge. She waved back.

A cool wind blew across the park. She

turned, looked toward the dirt lot where the Blazer was parked. On the far side, a gray Toyota with Florida plates sat beneath a live oak, away from the other vehicles, a figure in shadow behind the wheel. She couldn't tell if it was a man or woman. A parent maybe, listening to the radio, out of the wind, while their child rode the carousel.

Danny called to her as he came past again, the horse rising and falling lazily. *Love you, kid,* she thought. Then the carousel took him around again and out of sight.

Morgan watched them from the stolen car.

The woman had been easy to find. He'd taken the Toyota from the lot of an outlet mall near Arcadia, switched plates with another car, then driven down here. He'd gone to the sheriff's office first, parked in a strip mall across the street. On the seat beside him was a newspaper clipping with photos of the woman and Flynn. A little after five, he'd watched her pull her cruiser into the lot.

He got a better look when she left, still in uniform. Midthirties maybe, a good shape, brown hair tied up behind. She'd gotten into a silver Blazer, and he'd followed at a safe distance. First to her house, where he'd parked down the block, watched her go in and then come back out in street clothes, with a little boy. Then here to the park.

The carousel slowed, children getting off, others getting on. The boy ran toward her, and she scooped him up in her arms and hoisted him onto her shoulders, the way a father might, holding on to his ankles. They crossed the lot to the Blazer. As they got closer, Morgan saw there was something wrong with the boy. He was too thin, his hair sparse and uneven. When she set him down, he looked spent, had to hold on to her while she opened the back door, helped him up and into a booster seat.

*He's sick,* Morgan thought. *Something bad. Something that won't go away.*

As the woman got behind the wheel, she looked across at Morgan. He knew he was far enough from the streetlamp that she couldn't make him out, if she could see him at all.

He watched them drive off. He didn't need to follow. He knew where she lived now, what she drove.

Tomorrow he would find Flynn.

# FIFTEEN

Morgan parked the Toyota on a fire road, out of sight of the highway, and walked a quarter mile to where the woods ended and the dead cornfield began.

It was dusk, the shadows thickening around him. Across the cornfield, he could see lights go on in the house. It had taken him twenty minutes to find it, out here in the middle of nowhere, and he'd driven by twice, feeling exposed, before doubling back and finding this spot.

He wore a black windbreaker he'd bought in Arcadia, had zipped it halfway to cover the Beretta in his belt. He'd run the air conditioner in the car, but here in the open he was sweating under the pullover, his hands clammy inside the cotton work gloves.

As it grew darker, the woods seemed to come to life around him. The chirping of crickets everywhere, louder noises he didn't recognize. He found himself touching the

Beretta through his jacket.

From the edge of the trees, the ground sloped down to the cornfield, giving him a clear view of the front and back of the house. A pickup truck and an old Camaro were parked in the carport.

The front door opened, and a woman came out. Late thirties, blond hair, one side braided, black T-shirt, jeans. She stood in the yard, turned back to speak to a man in the doorway. Jeans and white T-shirt, curly hair. Flynn.

The woman got behind the wheel of the Camaro, started the engine. The noise was loud, ragged, the telltale cough of a bad muffler. Flynn went back in, closing the door behind him.

When she pulled out of the carport, Morgan walked back through the woods to the car.

It was easy to pick her up again. Once back on the main road, it wasn't long before he saw the distinctive shape of the Camaro's taillights ahead. Little traffic, easy to keep her in sight without getting close. He thought he'd lost her on a rise once, then saw the Camaro parked outside a package goods store. He'd driven by, pulled onto the shoulder a half mile later, doused the lights. Five minutes later, the Camaro passed him. After a few moments, he pulled out after it.

They were heading west, farther away from town, nothing but woods out here. He followed at a distance, saw her slow, make a left, seem to disappear into the trees.

He drove by and saw the road there, the billboard for the housing development. There was a phone number on it, a drawing of a town house, an orange arrow that pointed down the road.

A half mile ahead, he pulled onto the shoulder and swung the Toyota back around. As he neared the side road, he killed the lights, made the turn.

The road was newly paved, the curbs marked with yellow chalk, spray-painted red arrows where the gas lines were. The trees gave way to condo units in varying degrees of construction, empty lots between them, all the buildings dark. He slowed, not wanting to come up on her if she'd pulled to the side of the road.

He passed a backhoe and bulldozer parked in a cleared lot. Ahead on his left, in one of the completed units, he could see light in a window, the Camaro parked at the curb outside.

He turned onto a side street, parked,

untwisted the wires that dangled from the broken steering column, killed the engine. He used an elbow to break the plastic cover of the dome light, pulled the bulb out. Then he took the roll of reflector tape from the hardware store bag and got out.

He cut through yards, all the houses empty, no one else living here yet. As he neared the lighted unit, he could hear music inside. Empty lots on both sides, no streetlight out front.

Kneeling behind the Camaro, shielded from the house, he tore off a two-inch strip of tape. He picked a spot low on the bumper, brushed it clean, flattened the tape there, pressing until it held. At night, in the reflection of headlights, it would be easy to spot.

He put the roll of tape in his jacket pocket, slipped the Beretta out of his belt. He went up into an empty yard, coming up on the house from the right side. There was an attached garage there, a window. He looked in. In the lightspill from an open door he could see a blue Navigator with Palm Beach County plates. He tried the window. Unlocked.

He moved to the back of the house. The music was louder here, a thumping bass line. Reggae. There was a redwood deck, sliding glass doors with vertical blinds, lights on inside.

A side window cast a square of light on the dirt. He found a discarded cinder block, set it down, climbed up. No blinds or curtains. He was looking into a small dining room, a living room beyond. No furniture except for an old blue couch and a table lamp on the hardwood floor.

The woman sat on the couch, looking up at a light-skinned black man swaying in the center of the room, dancing by himself. He had thick dreadlocks tied back in a ponytail, wore a sleeveless T-shirt and loose fatigue pants that exposed two inches of flat stomach. He drew on a spliff, blew smoke out, still moving to the music. There was a boom box on the floor, plugged into a wall socket, a six-pack of Michelob beside it.

The woman spoke, and the man passed her the spliff. She drew deeply on it. He held out his hand and she took it, let him pull her off the couch. They began to dance, close, slow, their hips inches apart.

There was an ashtray on the arm of the couch, and he set the spliff in it and turned back to the woman. She was still dancing, eyes closed. He caught her braids, twisted them roughly so her neck bent. He kissed her then, openmouthed, and she ground against him.

When the kiss ended, she stepped back, pulled the T-shirt over her head. She was braless, and he leaned to suck her breasts while she worked at her belt. When it was loose, she pushed the jeans down, kicked them away. She knelt on the couch, facing away from him, her hands gripping the back of it. She looked over her shoulder, braids half-covering her face, spoke to him. He moved behind her, started to loosen his pants.

Morgan stepped down, picked up the cinder block, put it back where he'd found it. He could hear their noises inside, loud, even over the music. He walked back to the car.

He was still parked there, the cell on the seat beside him, when Mikey called back.

"C-Love gave me your message," Mikey said. "What up?"

"These Haitians. How well you know them?"

"C-Love did the meeting. He handled the details. Why?"

"You trust them?"

"What you mean?"

"Would they rip you? Set up the deal, then take your boy down?"

A pause. Mikey thinking about it.

"No," he said. "That don't make sense. Those boys are businessmen. What I sent was a down payment, that's all. There was more coming. A *lot* more. Why they want to mess that up?"

"I don't know."

"And why fuck with me anyway? They know that shit would come back on them."

"Maybe they thought all the heat on you right now, you wouldn't be able to do anything."

Another pause.

"Nah. Like I said, don't make sense. They got so much shit coming in down there, they don't know what to do with it. Why cut off a market? And why leave the guns? No banger ever walked away from a machine gun."

"I guess you're right."

"Why you ask?"

"Just wondering," Morgan said. "I'm down here, and that cop who shot Willis? His girlfriend's got a taste for the dark. She's holed up with him right now."

"Haitian?"

"Could be."

"Motherfucker."

"Maybe it's not connected," Morgan said.

"Maybe she just likes a little strange on the side."

"Maybe you need to have a talk with that boy."

"That's what I was thinking."

"Let me send the twins, man. This shit is getting complicated."

"No need for that. I'll tell you if there is."

"They ready when you need them."

*I'm sure they are,* Morgan thought, *and ready to get their hands on that money, too.*

"No," he said. "It's under control."

"Keep it that way, brother," Mikey said and ended the call.

# SIXTEEN

Sara signed on to the computer, got the keyword prompt, typed in "Taurus revolver," hit RETURN.

Three hits, links to reports. The first was the Willis shooting. She clicked on the second, waited for it to come up. It was a case from a year ago that she remembered, an attempted armed robbery at a gas station, the suspect dropping the weapon as he fled. She wrote the evidence control number on a pad.

The third link was a domestic violence case from two years ago. Three guns had been seized as part of a restraining order — a Smith and Wesson .38 Chiefs Special, a Colt .45 automatic, and a Taurus revolver — but the Taurus was logged as being a .357. She wrote down the number anyway, did a fresh search on "Taurus" with no qualifiers, found nothing else. She signed off, tore the top sheet from the pad.

The Evidence Control Room was in the basement. A long, institutional-green corridor, pipes running along the ceiling, fluorescent lights hanging below them. There was a window halfway down the hall, a closed door beside it.

Charlie Stern was at the window, writing on a clipboard. She could hear his faint wheezing. He was in his late fifties but looked ten years older, his belly sloping over his belt, his flattop solid white.

" 'Lo, Sara," he said.

"Charlie, I'm wondering if you can help me with something."

He looked at her, then at the clock on the wall behind him. "Five forty-five."

"I know. This will only take a couple minutes."

After six, when Charlie left, anyone wanting access to Evidence had to go through the sheriff. She didn't want that.

"What have you got?" he said.

She handed him the slip of paper. "I need to see the weapons under these numbers. I'm looking for a Taurus, .38 caliber."

"What's this about?"

"Case I'm working. Just need to make sure they're accounted for."

"Hold on," he said and left the window.

She waited. Through the window she

could see rows of metal shelving rising to the ceiling, brown banker's boxes. She could hear his breathing, his slow, heavy footsteps.

Five minutes later, he came back to the window, put two heavy plastic evidence bags on the sill, got his clipboard.

"You'll need to sign these out," he said.

"I just need to look. Only take a minute."

She opened the bags, looked at the weapons inside. The first was the .38, with cracked walnut grips. The second was bigger, the .357, nickel plated. Both had yellow plastic cord threaded through the barrels and cylinders.

"Let me ask you something, Charlie."

He raised an eyebrow. She could sense his impatience.

"When did we start computerizing all our evidence, logging it in?"

He shrugged.

"Nineteen ninety-nine maybe. They had a clerk in here for a while, backlogging the hard copies into the computer, but I don't know how far back she got. Couple years maybe, why?"

"If I was looking for a weapon taken as evidence before that, how would I find it?"

"Well, if you knew the case file number, I could track it that way. Everything back here is in order, more or less. I need to go soon,

Sara. Can this wait?"

She smiled at him.

"I'm sorry," she said. "But as long as I'm down here . . . if you could just help me out a little."

"We used to keep logs, hard copy, of all the weapons moved into Evidence. That's before my time, though."

"You still have them?"

He sighed, then touched a button under the window. The door buzzed open. "Come on in."

When she went through, he shut the door behind her, pulled the grate down over the window, secured it with a padlock.

"Last thing I need is someone else coming along," he said. "They're over here."

On one side of the room was a desk and wall shelves stacked with ledger books.

"Each of those covers about four years," he said. "None of them are in the computer yet."

She took the first book down, dusted her sleeve along the spine — 1986–1990.

She nodded at the desk chair. "You mind?"

"Go ahead," he said. "I've got paperwork to finish up." He went back to the window and the clipboard.

The desktop was cluttered with papers.

Near the phone was a half-eaten cheese sandwich on white bread. A fly crawled along its edge. She sat, opened the book on her lap.

It was set up like a standard financial ledger, headings for each year, then each month, tabbed columns. Most of the entries were in blue ink, some in green or red. The same spidery hand throughout. Charlie's predecessor, whoever that had been. Each entry had a case number.

She ran her fingers down the tabs, looking at the annotations. *Shotgun, 12-gauge, single-shot. Colt .45, Peacemaker. Star .25.* All weapons that had been seized during or after a crime. She stopped every time she came to a .38. Smith and Wesson. Rugers. Dan Wessons. No Taurus.

She turned pages, scanned columns, her nose itching from the dust.

"How we doing back there, Sara?"

"Okay, Charlie. Sorry about this."

"Let me know when you're done." Resignation in his voice.

She found it on the sixth page. March 1988. A Taurus .38, seized in a motor vehicle stop. The serial number was written down. At the end of the column, the case number.

She opened desk drawers. There was a

*Penthouse* in the top one, an inhaler. She opened the second, found a blank sheet of SO stationery. She wrote down the two numbers.

"Charlie?" she called out.

"You want to tell me what this is all about, Sara?"

They'd found the box. It was on the fourth rack up, three aisles back, and Sara had pulled the sliding ladder over, climbed up herself. Charlie seemed grateful. He stood beside her, looking up, breathing heavy.

She pulled the box off the shelf, backed down the ladder carefully, Charlie steadying it for her.

"Thanks," she said and carried the box to the desk. Before taking the lid off, she checked the case numbers written on the front — 01404 to 01411. She was looking for 01408.

There were six evidence bags in the box, each with a case number written on the plastic. She went through them carefully. Clothes, a Buck knife, a .25 automatic. No Taurus, and no bag that matched the case number.

"What's wrong?" Charlie said.

"Anybody check anything out of here

recently, Charlie?"

"Not when I was around. That far back, why would anyone want to? Those cases are long closed, and if they weren't, they won't ever be."

She fit the lid back on.

*It doesn't mean anything. Things get misfiled all the time. Probably half the things down here are misfiled.*

"Okay," she said. "All set."

"Good."

She went up the ladder again, slid the box back into the cleared space in the dust. She climbed down, brushed the front of her uniform.

"You all right?" Charlie said. "You look like you're not so happy all of the sudden."

"It's okay," she lied. "Turned out to be nothing after all."

He looked at her for a moment, then went around the room switching off lights. The overhead fluorescents hummed, blinked, and went dark.

She followed him into the corridor. He locked the door behind them.

"One other thing, Charlie?"

"What?"

"Don't tell anyone about this, okay? It's just something I had to see for myself."

"If you say so," he said and held the

stairwell door for her.

Back upstairs, she changed in the ladies' room, bundled her uniform and vest into her tac bag. When she got out to the parking lot, Billy was leaning against the hood of the Blazer. His truck was parked behind it.

She stopped.

"Hey, Sara."

He wore jeans, a flannel shirt, looked like he hadn't slept.

She didn't move.

"I didn't want to come out to the house again," he said. "I didn't know if I'd be welcome."

"What do you want?"

"To talk."

"About what?"

"Not out here, Sara. Not like this."

She looked back at the front door. Hoped someone would come out, see them together.

"I was thinking about the other night," he said. "I didn't like the way we left things."

"Not the time, Billy. I need to go, Danny's waiting."

"Maybe you could call JoBeth, ask her to stay a little later. Then we could get a drink, talk."

"I don't think so."

"Has your opinion of me changed that much? We can't even have a friendly drink anymore?"

"You look like hell, Billy. And you shouldn't be here anyway."

"Did Danny like the dinosaur model?"

"He did."

"Just one drink, Sara. I just want to talk. Can't you give me that?"

She looked at her watch, then back at him.

"Twenty minutes. That's all."

"Good enough." He gestured to his truck.

"I'll follow you," she said.

"Don't want to drive with me?"

"You want to talk or not?"

"Sorry. Whatever you want," he said.

"If I lose you, I'll see you there."

"Not Tiger's. Not tonight."

"Where?"

"Somewhere else. I'll find a place."

"Not far."

He nodded, moved toward his truck.

She got behind the wheel, set the tac bag on the passenger seat. She watched him pull out of the lot, the truck bouncing as a tire went over the curb.

She followed him, opened the bag, took out the leather Cordura waistpack she sometimes wore. She pulled the Velcro breakaway tab that opened the front pocket.

Steering with one hand, she took the Glock from the tac bag, tugged it free of its holster. She slid it into the waistpack, closed the Velcro.

As they got farther from town, heading west, she noticed the gray Toyota about three car lengths back, moving at a steady speed, not closing the distance. Something about it jogged her memory, but she couldn't place where she'd seen it before.

*Or maybe you're just getting paranoid.*

In the half-light of dusk, with the Toyota's headlights on, the figure behind the wheel was only a shadow. Four miles later, the car was still there. She slowed, but it didn't try to pass.

Ahead, Billy had moved into the far right lane, was signaling to turn. She put her blinker on, followed. The Toyota pulled into the left lane, sped up. As it passed, she caught a glimpse of a black man at the wheel. Then just the glow of the Toyota's taillights, down the road and gone.

# SEVENTEEN

They ended up in a bar on the far edge of the county, one she'd never been to before. Mostly Indians in here, up from the Seminole Reservation in Immokalee, all men. Sara felt self-conscious as their eyes lingered on her. The jukebox was playing Tammy Wynette, and the ceiling fans were doing nothing to reduce the hanging haze of cigarette smoke.

When she came in, Billy was already at a booth in the back, a cypress table marked with cigarette burns. He looked at her, at the waistpack she wore.

"I won't ask what's in there," he said.

She slipped into the booth. "I don't have a lot of time."

He got up. "No waitresses here."

He went to the bar. Sara looked around. A middle-aged Indian in a western shirt, hair slicked back, turned on his stool to look at her, smiling drunkenly. *Christ,* she thought. *What am I doing here?*

Billy came back to the table with a pitcher and two mugs.

"PBR," he said. "All they had on tap."

He sat down, poured.

"I would have asked for Guinness," he said, "but I don't think they have much call for it out here."

"I'm not here to drink."

"I know." He slid a filled mug in front of her, looked at his own. "Like I said, I feel bad about the way we left things."

She looked away, her patience fading. The Indian was still watching her. She stared at him, didn't look away, and he shrugged finally, turned back to the bar.

"You feel differently about me now," Billy said. "I know that. It can't ever be what it used to be."

"We don't need to go into all this, Billy. There's no reason."

"When you're a kid, sometimes you let things get away from you, you know? You're twenty-five, thirty, it's easy to say, 'Yeah, it didn't work out.' Like there's always another opportunity, someone else coming down the line. Get to be my age and you realize you're running out of options. And sometimes the things you let get away from you are the things you should have held on to with both hands."

She met his eyes.

"My age, you let something go and you end up wondering if that was the one," he said. "That you let it go and you're never going to get it back."

"I wasn't the one, Billy. Get that out of your head. If I was, we wouldn't be in this situation. You made your own decisions. You can't blame them on anyone else."

"I know that. It's just that with you . . ." He looked away. "I just got scared, I guess. You, Danny. The way he is. I tried to be there, you know? Be strong. But sometimes I just couldn't handle it."

"I've heard that before."

"What do you mean?"

"When Roy left, right after Danny got sick. That's one of the things he told me. He loved Danny so much, he couldn't stay around and watch him die. You know what that meant? That meant he was a fucking coward. And Danny's still here. He's not dying, and he's going to get better, and I'll do whatever I have to do to make that happen. Roy couldn't handle Danny? That was his excuse. He couldn't handle anything."

He looked at his beer.

"You were his friend, Billy. You knew him.

You know what I'm talking about."

He nodded without looking up.

"Go ahead and drink that if you want," she said. "I don't care."

"You've got a right to be mad, I understand that."

"Do you?"

"And you're right, some of the choices I made weren't the best."

"I'm not your therapist, Billy."

"I know. But sometimes I think you were the only real chance I had to be happy, to have a normal life. And I let it slip away."

"You've had lots of opportunities to be happy," she said, "and they've got nothing to do with me. That's your own responsibility. You can't put it on other people."

"You're right. But lately things have gotten . . . complicated. Sometimes it seems like everything's so fucked I'll never get out from under."

"What do you mean?"

He shook his head. She sensed him pulling back. *Give him space, let him talk.*

She sat back, lifted the mug, and sipped beer. It was thin, harsh. She frowned, put it down. Johnny Paycheck on the jukebox now, "Take This Job and Shove It."

"They're telling me I'm clear," he said. "That it was all in policy."

"That's right."

"They look at me differently now, though. You do, too."

"I don't know what you mean."

"Elwood came out to the house the other day." He looked at her. "To talk to Lee-Anne, when I wasn't there. She had nothing to tell him, but still . . . I mean, if it's open and shut, it's open and shut, right?"

"Maybe they want to make sure all the *T*s are crossed. For your sake."

"Or maybe it's just that nigger woman stirring up trouble."

"I don't think I've ever heard you use that word before."

"Dammit, Sara, I just —"

"I have to go, Billy. Thanks for the beer." She started to get up.

"I know you still care about me, Sara." He looked at her. "Everything we've had between us. The other night, too. I know you get angry with me sometimes, but you're still on my side, even though things didn't work out. I know that. I can feel it."

She squeezed out of the booth. "I have to go home. You should, too."

"I think I'm going to stay here a little bit. Drink some of this beer. Enjoy the change of scenery. At least out here I don't have to worry about anyone spying on me, do I?"

"Good night, Billy."

"Good night, Sara. I don't blame you. I really don't."

She turned her back on him, headed toward the door.

Midnight, the house dark except for the kitchen light. She sat in the living room in sweats and sneakers, running it all through her head. The conversation with Billy. The missing Taurus. The gray Toyota that had followed her. *Or maybe not. Maybe it's just you.*

Headlights came through the blinds, crawled across the walls, and were gone. She went to the window, pushed the blinds aside, looked out. It had rained earlier, and now there was mist in the air, a hazy halo around the streetlamps. She saw taillights at the end of the street, turning right and then disappearing.

She went down the hall, checked on Danny. He lay still under the covers. She stood in the doorway for a moment, until she could hear his soft snores.

Another set of headlights swept across the living room, this time from the opposite direction. They seemed to slow for a moment, hang motionless on one wall, and then move on. By the time she got to the window, they were gone.

She got her hooded sweatshirt from the hall closet, pulled it on. The only sound in the house was the ticking of the kitchen clock. In the bedroom, she took the Glock from the lockbox and slipped it into the front pocket of the hoodie, the weight of it hanging heavy.

She went out the back door, down the two short steps, and into the sideyard. The air was thick and damp. She started toward the front of the house, stopped to listen. Nothing except the sound of a TV from the upper window of the house next door.

Headlights again, to her right, slower this time. They pulled up a block away on the opposite side of the street, then winked out. She could hear the low thrum of an idling engine.

She slipped the Glock out, staying close to the wall. At the corner of the house, she stopped. Through the mist she could see only a dim bulk across the street, yards from the nearest streetlight. She wished she'd brought her shield. She'd walk over, gun up, badge whoever it was, be done with it.

Moisture dripped from the gutter above her. She waited, watching. She thought of Danny inside.

*Fuck it. Badge or no.*

She left the cover of the house and started down the lawn, the Glock in a two-handed grip, pointed at the ground. She heard the crunching of gears, the sound of wet tires.

"Police! Don't move!" she yelled, the Glock coming up even before she reached the sidewalk. "Turn that vehicle off."

It pulled hard away from the curb before she reached the street, lights still off, tires squealing. She saw only a blur in the mist as it went past. It reached the end of the street, turned right at the stop sign without slowing. As it did, it passed through the lightwash of a streetlamp. Black pickup, mud flaps. Billy's truck.

She lowered the Glock and walked back to the house through the mist.

# EIGHTEEN

When the man with the dreadlocks came into the garage, Morgan put the muzzle of the Beretta to the back of his head.

"One in the chamber," he said. "You know what that means, right?"

The man froze. Morgan pushed him toward the Navigator.

"Hands on the hood."

He did as he was told. He was bare chested in jeans, his dreads loose, a blue bandana tied around his neck. He smelled of reefer.

Morgan used his left hand to pat the man's pockets, took out a wallet. He put it in the windbreaker.

"Anyone else in the house?" Morgan said.

He shook his head.

"Answer me."

"No, no one." A faint accent.

"If there is," Morgan said, "I'll shoot you first." He took the gun away. "Turn around.

Go back in."

The man took his hands off the hood, turned to look at Morgan, the gun. His face was slack with fear. "I don't know what you want, brah, but there's nothing here."

"Go on," Morgan said.

He went up the steps into an empty kitchen. Morgan followed, pulled the connecting door shut. On the counter were a cell phone and a big automatic, a Desert Eagle .44. The back door was locked and chained. Morgan opened another door, saw steps that led into a basement, listened, heard nothing. The man watched him.

"Living room," Morgan said.

They went in. The sliding glass door was closed, the vertical blinds drawn. A tall straight-backed chair was against one wall.

"What is this place?" Morgan said.

"How you mean?"

"Who lives here?"

"No one yet. A friend of mine, he sells these places. He's letting me stay here."

"Face the couch."

When he did, Morgan hit him hard on the side of the head with the Beretta. He cried out, fell to his knees. The floor lamp threw his shadow large on the wall.

"Stay there," Morgan said and backed away. He put the Beretta in his belt, took out the wallet. Inside was a hundred dollars in cash, credit cards in three different names. A Florida driver's license with a picture, in the name of Jean-Pierre Delva, a Riviera Beach address. He tossed the wallet on the couch.

Delva had a hand to his head, blood coming through his fingers. "There's nothing here for you, man. That's all the money I got."

In the kitchen, the cell began to play music, a tune Morgan didn't know. Delva looked up.

"Who is that?" Morgan said.

"I don't know."

Morgan could sense his nervousness.

"Your girlfriend?"

"Who?"

"The white girl. The one that was here last night."

The tune played for a few seconds, stopped.

"Her boyfriend know about you two?"

"What boyfriend?"

"Flynn. The deputy."

"I've got lots of women, man. Maybe he know, maybe he don't. Why you ask me?"

"Get up," Morgan said. "Sit down over there."

He rose unsteadily, settled into the

wooden chair, looked at his bloody hand, all the fight gone from him.

"Where's the money?" Morgan said.

"What money, brah?"

The cell phone rang again. They both looked toward the kitchen. The tune stopped.

Morgan took the Beretta back out.

"I've come a long way," he said. "You think I'm just going to walk out of here?"

Delva looked at him. "You from up north, right? You work for that fat man."

"I don't work for anybody."

"I can't help you, man. I don't have it."

"But you know who does."

"Talk to the woman. She knows. They told me nothing."

"But you helped set it up, right? So you've got a share coming."

"I passed along some things I'd heard. That's all."

"And now they're holding out on you? Making you wait?"

Delva looked at the floor.

"Who put it together? You, the girl, Flynn. Who else?"

"What do you mean?"

"The other deputy, the woman. Was she part of it?"

"I don't know who that is, who you're

talking about."

From outside, the sound of a car engine, low. Morgan looked into the front room. Big windows there, with blinds. No headlights outside. The engine sound faded.

"We have to get out of here," Delva said.

"Why?"

"They've been looking for me. These boys down here don't play. They coming to talk."

"About the money? Why they never got it?"

Delva didn't answer.

Morgan went into the front room, looked out the window. There was a single streetlight down the block, mist hanging around it. The street was empty.

"They'll come back," Delva said.

Morgan looked at his watch. Ten minutes after midnight.

"Get up," he said. "You're coming with me."

The phone chimed again. Morgan backed into the kitchen and picked it up, still watching Delva. He opened the phone, lifted it to his ear.

"Yo, *papi* why you not answering?" A thick island accent. "We outside, boy. Let us up in there. We need to talk, *konprann?*"

Morgan looked at the sliding glass door, at the dining room window. A shadow passed by it. He'd waited too long. He wondered how many of them were outside.

"You there, *gason?* Don't fuck around."

He closed the phone, dropped it on the counter.

"What are you doing?" Delva said.

Two bangs at the back door, someone rattling the knob.

*"Louvri la pot!"*

Footsteps on the deck.

Morgan started toward the front door. It would be his best chance. If he ran, he could lose them in the night, make it back to where he'd parked the Toyota. They'd be too busy with Delva to chase him.

The sliding door exploded. Glass showered inward, a cinder block skidding across the wood floor. A figure pushed the blinds aside to come through, and Morgan fired twice, sent it reeling back onto the deck. He put another shot into the darkness beyond, then swiveled and aimed at the dining room window, the shadow that had reappeared there. He fired, blew glass out.

There was silence then. Delva was on the floor, using the couch for cover. Shards of glass fell from the frame of the sliding door, broke on the floor. He could hear them out there, getting ready to try again. Time to move.

He went to the front door, fired through it in case someone was on the other side. He worked the locks, kicked the screen door open, went out fast and low. He heard shouting to his left, fired in the direction of it, and then his foot hit wet grass and slid out from under him and he went down onto his side.

He grunted with the impact, heard shots popping behind him, gunfire from inside the house. He got to his feet, half sprinted, half slid down the slope of lawn to the street. Shouts behind him, more shots. He twisted, saw two men in the doorway, blue bandanas around their necks, guns pointing at him. One of them called out, "Andre! Andre! Get him! *Vit!*"

Morgan fired at them, blew off a piece of door frame. They ducked back inside.

He started to run, away from the street-light, then saw the dark shape of the car parked ahead. A man was coming around it fast, an automatic in his hand. Ten feet between them, no cover. They raised their guns at the same time, and Morgan saw the blocky shape of the Russian pistol, heard the click. Then another.

The man lowered the gun, pulled on the slide. Jammed. Morgan shot him twice in the chest.

More shouts from the house. Morgan ran past the car, across the street. A shot whined off the pavement to his left. He kept running, saw the empty lot a block away, the construction equipment.

When he reached the bulldozer, he swung behind it and sat down in the dirt, his back against the treads. He was breathing hard, tightness spreading across his chest, a solid ball of pain in his right side.

Muffled shouts. A car starting. He pressed back against cold metal, the damp ground soaking through his pants.

Headlights, engine noise. Beams lit up the empty ground to his left. They'd have the windows down, weapons out, looking for movement.

The car passed, the ground going dark again. His breathing was starting to slow, the pressure in his stomach and sides easing.

After a few minutes, the car came back from the other direction. Headlights played across the bulldozer blade. He gripped the Beretta, wondering if they had the courage to get out of the car, look for him on foot.

The car rolled by. The shadows around him turned back into darkness.

How long he sat there, he didn't know. After a while, he heard the car again, coming from the direction of the house. It went past the bulldozer without slowing, engine noise fading in the night.

He looked at his watch. One forty. He tried to stand, his legs stiff, had to sit again. It was easier the second time, one hand braced against the muddy tread. He heard his knees pop.

He set the Beretta on the bulldozer seat, looked back toward the house. Light in the windows still. No car out front.

He rubbed his legs until feeling returned. The next time he checked his watch, it was two.

He started back, the Beretta at his side. His knees and hips ached, but the stomach pain had subsided. He crossed through backyards and empty lots until he was opposite the house. No sound or movement from inside.

No body in the street, just a glistening on the pavement where it had been. He went across fast, then along the side of the garage. The Navigator was still there.

He went around back and onto the deck, listened for a moment, and then stepped through the shattered door and twisted blinds. The living room was empty. He checked the other rooms quickly. No one.

The gun and cell were gone from the

kitchen counter. The cellar door was closed. He'd left it open when he'd checked it earlier.

He raised the Beretta, twisted the doorknob, pushed. Hc pointed the gun down the steps into blackness. No sound below, no movement.

He felt for the light switch, tripped it, illuminated wooden steps, a concrete floor. Went down slowly, gun up, the steps creaking.

Delva was in the center of the basement. They'd brought the chair down, tied him to it, clothesline knotted around his chest. He was slumped forward, naked, dreadlocks hanging over his knees. His jeans lay on the floor a few feet away. Below the chair, a pool of dark and drying blood. Morgan could smell the copper tang of it.

He pointed the Beretta at him, moved closer, knew what he'd find. There was an entry wound behind his left ear, the dreads there matted with blood.

Near the chair, a set of bloody pruning shears. Delva's left arm dangled almost to the floor, but the pinkie and ring fingers were stumped, blood spatter on the concrete beneath them. The blue bandana was tied tight around his wrist, a makeshift tourniquet to keep him from bleeding out while they worked on him.

Morgan put a gloved finger on his forehead, gently pushed. The mouth sagged open and something fell out, bounced from a naked thigh to clatter on the floor. A black domino with six white circles.

Morgan went back up the steps, turned the light off, closed the door.

He'd parked the Toyota in a stand of scrub pine three blocks away, hidden from the street. The night was quiet around him. As he neared the car, he raised the Beretta, in case they'd found it, were waiting for him. No one.

He got in, touched wires to restart the engine. Then he reversed out of the trees, cut the wheel hard, started back.

He was shirtless in front of the mirror, wiping sweat with a towel, when the cramp hit him.

It bent him, a stabbing pain followed by a burning surge through his bowels. He tore at his belt, got the pants down and made it onto the toilet just in time. The waste exploded out of him, hot and fluid and painful, spasm following spasm. He put his elbows on his knees, rested his head in his hands. He felt dizzy, flush.

After a while, the pain lessened. He sat

there until the nausea subsided, then cleaned himself off and turned on the shower. He stood in the lukewarm spray, holding on to the showerhead for balance.

When he was done, he dried off as best he could, drank a glass of cool water from the sink, splashed more on his face. He got a full Vicodin down, then checked the door locks and lay across the bed, feeling the room start to spin around him. It was five minutes before he had the energy to crawl under the sheet.

The last thing he did was take the Beretta from the nightstand and set it on the bed beside him, the grip cool in his sweating hand. Then he closed his eyes.

# NINETEEN

Sara spun the wheel and turned into Billy's driveway, dust kicking up around the Blazer. The Camaro and truck were both in the carport.

She braked, leaned on the horn. Eight thirty in the morning, but she'd been up most of the night. She hit the horn again, held it, saw curtains pushed aside in the kitchen window. *Woke them up. Good.*

The door opened, and Billy came out. Jeans, white T-shirt, flip-flops. Lee-Anne in the doorway behind him in cutoffs and Jack Daniel's T-shirt.

Sara opened her door, stepped down. He tried to smile as he got closer, his face still puffy from sleep, eyes bloodshot.

"Jesus, Sara," he said. "A little early for a Saturday, isn't it?"

She stepped to him, swung with her right hand, putting her hip into it as she'd been taught. Her fist cracked into his left cheek-

231

bone, snapped his head to the side. She felt the impact all the way to her shoulder. He stagger-stepped, recovered.

"What the *fuck,* Sara?"

She heard the screen door slam, turned to see Lee-Anne coming toward them.

"Keep your hands off him, bitch!"

Sara turned to face her, got ready.

Billy stepped between them, caught Lee-Anne's arm. "Whoah," he said.

She tried to push past him. Sara held her ground, waiting for her to close the distance. Billy used his body to turn Lee-Anne back toward the house. She twisted out of his grip.

"Who the *fuck* do you think you are?" Spittle flew from her mouth. "Don't you ever fucking touch him!"

He caught her arm again, tried to steer her away. "It's okay," he said. "Enough. It's okay."

She lunged, her face bright red, and Sara took an involuntary step back. Billy held her tight.

"Why can't you just leave us alone?" Lee-Anne said. "What's your fucking problem?"

Billy squeezed her arm, turned her gently.

"It's all right," he said. "We're just going to talk. Go back inside."

She pulled away from him, turned back to

Sara, but didn't come closer. Sara could feel her heart pumping, her face warm.

"Stay away from here. You come back again, deputy or no, I'll beat your dyke ass."

"Inside, Lee-Anne." He put a hand on her lower back to guide her. She pushed it away, and he slipped an arm around her waist, whispered in her ear, turned her back toward the house again.

They watched as she went up the stairs and inside, the screen door slamming behind her.

"I think you should leave," he said. "She means it."

"No chance. What were you doing outside my house last night?"

"I wasn't."

"No? Then who was driving your truck?"

He slipped his hands in his back pockets, turned to look at the house, then back at her. There was a red blotch on his cheek.

"Let's go somewhere we can talk," he said.

"What's wrong with here?"

"Not a good idea."

She looked past him, saw Lee-Anne standing behind the screen, watching them.

"Okay," Sara said. "Get in."

She K-turned and headed back down the driveway, trembling with adrenaline. When they reached the main road, she said,

"Where are we going?"

"Doesn't matter."

She turned left.

He touched his cheek, the redness already darkening into a bruise. "You still hit solid. Guess I deserved that, all I've put you through lately."

"You want to tell me what's going on?"

He looked out his window. They reached the highway intersection, turned toward town, neither of them speaking. Ahead on the right was the old Hopedale Diner, sign long gone, windows plywooded over. She pulled into the cracked lot. A rusted newspaper honor box lay on its side near the entrance.

She killed the engine, looked at him. He angled the rearview toward him, examined his cheek, the spreading bruise.

"I know about the Taurus," she said.

He pushed the mirror back, looked out the window.

"And?" he said.

"And it's time you start talking to me. What were you doing at my house?"

"I was worried about you."

"Worried about what?"

"A lot of things."

"Like how much I know?"

"Maybe."

"You need to tell me what's going on, Billy, before all this gets out of hand."

He powered down his window, looked at the diner's boarded-up entrance. "Would you believe me if I told you there was an explanation?"

"I'm listening."

"What do you know about the gun?"

"That it came from the evidence room at the SO. That you planted it on Willis."

"You're right." He met her eyes. "I did."

*There it is. So why are you not surprised?*

"Christ, Billy. Why?"

"Why do you think? I got scared."

"What happened out there? Really."

He took a breath.

"It was pretty much like I told it," he said. "He was speeding, wandering all over the road. I pulled him over, looked at his documents. He was nervous, so I asked him if there were any drugs or weapons in the car, anything I should know about. He said no, so I asked him to open the trunk. That's when he bolted."

"He was already out of the car?"

"He said the trunk release up front didn't work, he had to use the key. He went around back, as if he were getting ready to open it, then tossed the keys at my face, took off down the slope. I told him to stop, and when he turned around I saw a gun in his hand. At least I thought it was a gun. I drew and fired."

"What was it?"

"I don't know. When I got down there I couldn't find anything. I hunted around. I was sure I saw it, you know? But there was nothing. That's when I started to panic."

"You had the Taurus with you?"

"In a wheel well in the cruiser. I'd been carrying it for about a year, I guess. I'd heard it was what the old-timers used to do. Keep a throwdown handy, just in case."

"Thirty years ago maybe. If the sheriff had found out about it, you would have been fired."

"I know. I never thought I'd have to use it. I'd almost forgotten it was there."

"What did you do then?"

"I could tell he was dead, or close to it. The Taurus was already wiped clean, and I'd taken the numbers off it a long time ago. I climbed back down there, fit his hand around it, got his prints on it. Then I went back up to the cruiser and called it in, found the keys and opened the trunk, saw the bag there. That's when you came along."

"You should have told me the truth. You owed it to me."

"And if I had? Told you I'd used a throwdown, planted evidence? What would you have done?"

"I don't know."

"Kept it to yourself?"

"I don't know."

"I do. You wouldn't have. You're too good a deputy for that. You would have told El-wood or the sheriff. If not that night, then the next day, when you thought about it some more. I know you, Sara. You would have, and you know it."

"Maybe it would have been better off that way."

"Better off? He was black, Sara, and I'm white. You think I would have gotten a fair hearing, shooting an unarmed black man? FDLE would have been involved, the state attorney, the governor before it was over. Every minister in Libertyville would have been screaming for my head."

"You would have been cleared. They would have understood."

"You're dreaming. I would have been fired, at least. Criminal charges, more than likely. Maybe prison. And how do you think I'd make out there?"

"There had to be another way."

"Burned that bridge, Sara. There's no other way. Not now."

She watched a semi rumble past, raising dust.

"How long have you known about the gun?" he said.

"Since yesterday."

"You tell anyone about it?"

"No."

"Why not?"

She looked at him. "Why do you think?"

He looked out the windshield.

"If you want all this to go away, you need to face some things," she said. "You need to start telling the truth."

"It has gone away. At least that's what they're telling me." He looked at her. "The only one that can say different is you."

She couldn't meet his eyes, felt her anger, her momentum, slipping away. Somehow she'd lost the advantage, could feel it, knew he felt it, too.

"There were guns in the trunk, Sara. You saw them. He was no college kid."

"He was unarmed."

"I didn't know that. I'm sorry you got involved in all this. Sorry you had to be there. I never meant for any of this to happen. You have to believe that."

"I'm not sure what I believe anymore."

"What's that mean?"

She shook her head, watched cars go past.

"You know me better than anyone, Sara. What I had with you I never had with anyone else. Probably never will again."

"Don't."

"It's true. Whether you want to believe it or not."

"That's got nothing to do with this."

"It doesn't? I've told you everything, Sara. And only you. You want me in Raiford? Get out your phone, call the sheriff. I'll be in custody before the hour's over. Is that what you want?"

She didn't answer.

"Or maybe you're wearing a wire," he said, "and that's what this is all about."

She started the engine.

"You should get back," she said. "Lee-Anne will be waiting for you."

"What are you going to do?"

"I don't know."

"That's not good enough, Sara."

"It'll have to be."

He looked at her. "I can imagine the way you feel," he said. "The position I put you in."

"Can you?"

"If I could go back and change what happened that night, I would. But I can't bring him back. My going to prison won't change

239

that. I can't undo what was done. No one can."

"You're right about that. Go on, get out."

"What?"

"It's only about a mile back. You can walk it."

"I'm wearing sandals."

"I know." She looked at him. "Go on."

He opened the door, met her eyes for a moment, then climbed down.

"Tell me something," she said.

"What?"

"Have you ever told me the truth? Ever?"

"Don't be like that."

"About anything?"

They looked at each other for a moment. Then he shut the door.

"Billy."

He turned to face her through the open window.

"If I ever see you around my house again," she said. "If you come around me or Danny or anyone I know outside duty hours. . . ."

"You'll shoot me?"

She looked at him.

"I would never hurt you, Sara. You know that. Never could, never will. Danny either. But I'm wondering if you feel the same way."

After a moment, he turned and started for

the highway. In the rearview she saw him standing on the shoulder, waiting for a break in traffic.

She took out her cell, opened it, scrolled to Sheriff Hammond's home number. Her thumb lingered over the SEND button.

In the mirror, she saw Billy cross the highway to the opposite shoulder, start to walk along the grass there, heading home.

She closed the phone, tossed it on the passenger seat. Then she shifted into drive, pulled out of the lot.

For lunch, she made cold chicken sandwiches, reheated mashed potatoes. She took Danny's temperature while he sat at the table. When the thermometer beeped, he took it from his mouth, held it out to her. Ninety-nine point two. She felt his forehead.

"You feel all right?" she said.

"I'm okay. Just tired."

She gave him a baby Motrin to chew, poured him another glass of grape juice. After they ate, JoBeth cleared the table, and Sara went into the bathroom, closed the door, and ran the shower.

When the room filled with steam, she undressed and climbed into the too-hot stream, wincing at first. She closed her eyes, turned her face into the spray. Her hand was sore, the first two knuckles slightly swollen. She flexed her hand, eased some of the stiffness out, remembered what Billy has said.

*I can't undo what was done. No one can.*

They'd closed the case, made their findings public. Reopening it would mean trouble for everyone. Charges for Billy, prison likely. It would cost the sheriff his job, his pension. Maybe her job as well. Once the state was involved, it would be too late for damage control. It would be about scalps.

She sat in the tub, let the water wash over her and swirl down the drain, taking the morning with it. She pushed her hair back with both hands, closed her eyes.

If she did nothing, said nothing, it all ended right here. Right now. Their lives would go on.

*All you have to do is nothing. What could be easier than that?*

# TWENTY

Morgan woke tangled in sodden sheets. Bright light was coming in around the curtain edges. The nightstand clock told him it was three. He'd slept almost eleven hours.

Pushing the sheets away, he sat naked on the edge of the bed. His joints ached and his throat was swollen, his forehead warm to the touch. He realized he was shaking.

When he had the energy, he made his way into the bathroom, stood under the hot shower until the trembling stopped. Then he toweled dry, put the toilet seat down and sat there, head in his hands. *You have to get up,* he thought. *You have to keep moving.*

After a while, he went back into the room and got dressed. He stripped the sheets from the bed and pushed them into a pillowcase, along with the clothes from last night. He'd take them to the laundry room later, wash away the stale metallic smell that seemed to linger on everything he touched.

He opened the door, looked out. The sky was cloudless, the sun flashing off the Monte Carlo's windshield. He'd left the Toyota beside a collapsed barn off a rural road two towns away, out of sight, then walked to where he'd parked his car and driven back.

Birds chattered in the trees, and he could hear the rush of the creek. Far above, a plane left a white contrail across the sky.

He wiped a wrist across his slick forehead. A band of pain circled his skull. He couldn't afford to be sick, not now. Couldn't afford to lose a day.

He went back in, closed the door, opened the top panels to let air in. In the bathroom, he swallowed a Vicodin half, then went to lie on the bare mattress, looking up at the water-stained ceiling. After a while, he took the Beretta from atop the nightstand. He set it in his lap, the metal cold in his grip.

If it ever got too bad, if the pain was too much, if the doctors couldn't help him, this was what he would do. When his system began to shut down, when his skin turned ashen from the waste his kidneys couldn't process, this was how he would end it. Vicodin and then the gun. The cold muzzle against the roof of his mouth, his finger on the trigger.

He was sleeping again when the knock came. Then another, hard on the door frame. He woke with a start, and the Beretta slid from his lap, thumped on the floor.

The fever was gone, but he felt drained, weak. He pushed himself up, went to the curtains, looked out. A dark green Range Rover with tinted windows, New Jersey plates, was parked next to the Monte Carlo.

The knock came again, rattling the glass. He picked up the Beretta, held it at his side.

"Yo, man, open the door."

With his free hand, Morgan undid the dead bolt. He stepped back, his finger sliding over the Beretta's trigger.

"It's open," he said.

When Dante came into the room, Morgan shoved him hard toward the bed, swiveled and raised the Beretta. DeWayne stood framed in the doorway. When he saw the gun, he ducked fast to the right, out of sight.

Morgan kicked the door shut, turned to see Dante getting up off the floor. He grabbed the back of his basketball jersey, jerked him off balance again. As he fell into a sitting position, Morgan crouched behind him, left arm around his neck, put the muzzle of the Beretta to his temple.

"Hold on, man!" Dante said. "Hold the fuck on!"

"He comes through that door, you're going first."

"What the fuck you doing, man? Chill."

"Who's out there?"

"DeWayne."

"Who else?"

"No one."

Morgan tightened his grip. "Tell him to come in."

"I ain't telling him shit."

Morgan thumbed the hammer back for effect. "Tell him."

"Man, you don't want to do this."

Morgan screwed the muzzle into his skin.

Dante looked toward the door. "Yo, DeWayne," he called out. His voice was flat. "Come on in, it's cool."

The door cracked open. DeWayne looked around it into the room, left hand hidden behind his leg.

"Come in," Morgan said. "Slow."

The door opened wider.

"Let him go," DeWayne said, his voice a hoarse whisper.

"Whatever you've got back there, put it on the bed. Do it quick."

DeWayne's lazy eye twitched. He waited a long five count, then came into the room, tossed a chromed automatic onto the bare mattress.

"Shut the door," Morgan said.

He did, stood with his back to it.

Morgan loosened his grip on Dante's neck and got to his feet, his knees aching. He took a step back as Dante got his feet under him, adjusted his jersey. Morgan reached under the back of it, took out the small automatic he'd felt. He dropped it on the bed.

"Man, why you going off like this?" Dante said.

"What are you doing here?"

"Why you think?"

"I told him I didn't need anybody."

"I don't know what you told him. But he told *us* to come down here, hook up with you. So that's what we did."

Morgan decocked the Beretta. "You drive down?" he said.

"Just got here."

"We here to do work," DeWayne said. "Just like you."

He should shoot them both now, Morgan knew, leave them where they lay and head out. But then he would lose the motel as his base, bring in the police.

"Man wondering," DeWayne said. "Where you at with it."

"He should have called, saved you both a trip."

"He said for us to see for ourselves."

Morgan felt the adrenaline rush fading. He needed to sit down.

"Should have told me you were coming."

DeWayne raised his shoulders, let them fall.

Morgan nodded at the desk chair, said to Dante, "Sit down."

"You don't look so good," DeWayne said. "You all sweaty and shit."

"Don't worry about me," Morgan said, the words sounding weak and false. He went into the bathroom, put the Beretta on the toilet tank, ran the faucet and drank cold water from a cupped hand, splashed some on his face. He looked into the mirror. His eyes were sunken, his cheekbones showing through. The skull beneath his skin.

"Hotter than a motherfucker down here," Dante said. "I ain't used to this shit."

Morgan dried off with a towel, picked up the Beretta, went back into the room.

"Three's too many," he said. "No good. Especially down here. We stick out."

"Big Man said there's three or four of them you watching," Dante said. "That's why he sent us. Divide up the work, you know?"

"Don't need it."

"You want to call him, tell him different, go ahead. He tell us to go back, that's what we'll do. Until then . . ."

"So where you at with it?" DeWayne said.

Morgan looked at him. "If Mikey wants to know, I'll call him."

"Anything you wanna tell him, you can tell us."

"He say that?"

DeWayne nodded.

*And how much did he promise you?* Morgan thought. *A third? More? Or are you just planning to take it all?*

"These people you watching," Dante said. "They the ones got the money?"

"Maybe."

"You're not sure?"

"They the ones did Derek, though, right?" DeWayne said.

"Probably," Morgan said. "Why?"

"I been knowing Derek's people longtime. His father an OG. He watched out for me on the tier, you know what I'm saying?"

"That's got nothing to do with this."

"Derek was good people. They shouldn't have done him like that. I'll make sure that shit gets settled, you feel me?"

"You haven't thought this through."

"No thinking about it. Whoever did Derek

gonna get got."

"Money come first, though," Dante said. "Big Man down to stems and seeds. He need that cash."

"And then?"

Dante pulled at an earlobe. "Like the man said. Whoever did it got to go."

"That's what I mean, about not thinking this through. Think you can come down here, kill a cop, walk away?"

"A thieving-ass cop," DeWayne said.

"You think that makes any difference?"

"It should."

"We do it fast, then we git," Dante said. "We be gone before they know it. With the money."

Morgan felt fresh sweat on his forehead. The Beretta seemed heavier. He put it on the nightstand.

"You up to this?" DeWayne said. "You look like you about done."

"Where you staying?" Morgan said.

"Holiday Inn," Dante said. "Town or so over."

Used your own name, too, Morgan guessed. And after things jump off and the police start checking motels, they'll have that name, and an address, a description of the car, maybe a tag number. Stupid.

Morgan nodded at the guns.

"Pick them up," he said. "Mikey give you my cell?"

"We got it," Dante said.

"Go back to your room. Hit me on it later. I got a couple things to do first, get organized. Then we can talk about where it's going, how to divide it up. Don't do nothing until we talk."

"All right," Dante said. "Big Man calling the shots, though. You know that, right?"

"Up there, maybe."

"Down here, too."

Morgan said nothing. DeWayne opened the door.

"Later then," Dante said.

They got into the Range Rover, Dante behind the wheel. As it pulled away, Morgan could hear hip-hop thumping inside. He watched them head back down the access road to the highway. Then he went back inside to wait for the dark.

# TWENTY-ONE

They had an early dinner at the Dairy Queen, Danny picking at his hamburger, pushing fries around his plate. It was his favorite place to eat, and seeing him like this worried her. She reached across the table, put the back of her hand to his forehead. It was warm.

"You okay, little guy?"

He nodded, broke off a piece of hamburger, chewed it. The tyrannosaurus model was on his lap. He'd been carrying it all day.

She took another bite from her hamburger, realized she had no appetite. Her right hand was stiff, the knuckles still red.

She looked around the restaurant. Late Saturday afternoon and mainly teenagers in here, an elderly couple near the front window, the woman cutting up the man's food for him. There were decorations on the windows. Cutout jack-o'-lanterns, witches.

"Maybe a pirate," Danny said.

She looked at him. "I miss something?"

"For Halloween. I could be a pirate."

"Danny . . ."

"I know." He looked down at his food. "I was just thinking about it, that's all."

"You feel like you have a fever?"

He shook his head.

"Your hamburger okay?" she said.

He nodded.

"You have room for ice cream?"

He looked up. "Can I?"

"Try to eat a little more of that for me first, all right?"

He broke off another piece, chewed it. Her own hamburger was cold to the touch now.

When he'd eaten some more, she said, "That's okay, you don't have to finish it. Go on up, see what you want."

When he went to the counter, she cleared the table, dumped the uneaten food in the trash bin, and stacked their trays on top. They ordered small chocolate sundaes, and took them outside to the plastic tables near the parking lot. The sky was blue and clear. She watched a plane pass by far overhead.

"How would you like to go by the garage?" she said. "See Howard and Reno?"

"Can we?"

"You think you can handle it? It's pretty

hot today."

"Sure. I'm okay."

He scooped ice cream with the yellow plastic spoon, ladled into his mouth.

"How's your stomach?" she said. "You feel like you're going to be sick?"

He shook his head.

"Let me know if you are."

They finished their sundaes. She got rid of their trash, unlocked the Blazer, and opened the front and back doors to let the trapped heat out. As she helped him into the booster seat, he said, "I'm too old for this."

"Not yet. But soon."

When she had him secured, she got behind the wheel, started the engine, and cranked up the air-conditioning. He was playing with the tyrannosaurus, making growling noises, off in his own world.

Ten minutes later, they pulled into the lot at the Sunoco station that served as the Hopedale Municipal Garage. The flatbed was parked out front, along with two cruisers waiting to be repaired or picked up. Both bay doors were open, and she could see Howie Twelvetrees inside, standing under one of the lifts, looking up at the undercarriage of an EMT van.

He saw them, waved. A German shepherd/

mutt mix trotted out of the bay, ran a circle around the Blazer.

"Reno!" Danny said.

She shut the engine off, reached back, and got Danny unstrapped. He let himself out the side door, and the dog reared up, planted paws on his chest, almost knocking him back. He laughed, the dog licking at his face.

"Reno!" Howie said, coming out of the bay. "Easy."

The dog got down, flopped at Danny's feet. He scratched behind its ears, under its chain collar.

"Hey, Howie," she said as she got out.

He wiped his hands on a rag, slung it over the shoulder of his jumpsuit.

"Sara," he said. "So easy to look at, so hard to define."

He was in his late forties, she guessed, his complexion weathered by sun and wind. His jet black hair was lank and fell over one eye, his expression impassive. He could have been sixty for all she knew. She had never asked.

Reno had run back into the bay, come out with a cowhide pull toy, and dropped it at Danny's feet. He picked it up, hefted it over his shoulder, and tossed it across the black-top. The dog spun, streaked at it, caught it on the ground and carried it back, dropped it again.

"What can I do you for, Sara? Don't usually expect to see you on a Saturday."

"I was wondering if I could have a look at that Accord. The one from the shooting."

He looked at her, rubbed his hands on the rag. "Sheriff send you?"

She shook her head.

"I didn't think so," he said.

"Just curious about a couple things."

"Curious."

She waited.

"No harm in it, I guess," he said. He whistled sharply. "Reno! Back!"

The dog wheeled to face him, the toy in its mouth. It trotted up the short driveway and through the gate that led to the wrecking yard behind.

Howie led the way. The yard was high-fenced on three sides, chain link and barbed wire. There was a plywood doghouse against the back of the building. Reno dropped the toy, drank noisily from a plastic water dish.

There were three cars in the yard. A Ford station wagon with a crushed grille that Moss Harmon, the town's director of public works, had run into a cedarpost fence last month, half drunk. A VW Jetta that had been abandoned in Libertyville and impounded. Near the back fence was the gray Accord.

Danny squatted beside Reno. The dog finished drinking, picked up the toy again.

Sara walked around the Accord, remembering it that night, bathed in the light from their rollers. There were traces of white fingerprint powder on the doors, trunk, and hood.

"Locked?" she said.

Howie shook his head.

She opened the passenger side door. The rocker panels had been removed, dumped in the back. The safety seat was facedown on the floor, the back of it gone. She opened the door wider, saw the inside panels had been loosened. Wiring hung from beneath the dashboard.

"We took the whole thing apart," Howie said. "Sheriff's orders."

"Who's we?"

"Me and Sam Elwood. Sheriff dropped by to supervise for part of it."

"Find anything?"

"Where you going with this, Sara?"

"Like I said, just curious."

"Uh-huh."

"What are you worried about?"

"Me? Nothing."

"It's okay," she said. "I don't want to put

you on the spot. I'll ask the sheriff."

"Nothing personal, Sara."

She went around to the driver's side, pulled open the door. The console between thc scats had been dismantled. She knelt on the seat, leaned over and opened the glovebox. Empty.

"They took all that stuff," he said. "Registration, insurance, whatever else was in there. Sheriff's got it all."

"I guessed."

She backed out of the car.

"You looking for something specific?" he said.

"I'm not sure what I'm looking for."

"You have to be careful about what you're not looking for. Sometimes you find it."

"Don't go getting all Indian on me, Howie."

"One thing we did find, though."

"What's that?"

"Reach in and pop that trunk."

She looked at him a moment, then leaned back into the car and felt around under the left side of the seat. She found the trunk latch, pulled, heard the click.

"Come have a look at this," he said.

She followed him around to the trunk. He lifted the lid. It was empty inside, the carpet sagging in the middle.

"Where's the spare?" she said.

"We took it out, cut it open. What's left of it is in the shop. Nothing in it, though. Feel around behind that left taillight."

She did, tracing the wires to where they disappeared into the taillight mount.

"Up on the left," he said.

Her fingers found the small lever there.

"Pull it?" she said.

"Uh-huh."

She heard a click.

"Now lift up the carpet."

She did. A section of trunk bottom to the left of the spare well, about two feet across, had risen slightly.

"You could look at the floor of that trunk all day, not see it," Howie said. "Whoever built it did a good job."

She got her fingers under the edge, pulled. The section swung up on small hinges.

"It didn't roll out of the Honda factory that way," he said. "I can guarantee you that."

She looked into the space beneath. Bare metal. Empty.

"Anything in it when you opened it?"

"No. Just the way it is now."

"There were guns in the trunk when he pulled the car over," she said. "In plain sight."

"That's right."

"But nothing in here?"

"Nope."

She put her fingertips on the compartment lid, pressed it down so it clicked into place, flush with the trunk floor.

"Something, isn't it?" he said.

"It is."

"Doesn't make any sense, does it?"

"No."

"Didn't to the sheriff either."

"I wouldn't guess it did. Any fingerprints on it?"

"Wiped clean."

"Find anything else?"

"That's it."

"Thanks, Howie."

"If the sheriff asks if you've been around, what do I say?"

"Tell him the truth."

Behind her, Danny was laughing, in a tug-o'-war with Reno over the pull toy. The dog was winning, Danny giving ground inch by inch. She couldn't remember the last time she'd heard him laugh like that.

"Come on, honey," she said. "We need to go."

He released the toy and the dog fell backward, sprang up, and brought it to him again. He took her hand, rubbed the dog's head a final time. Howie walked them back to the Blazer.

"What's that?" he said.

"What?"

He knelt behind the rear bumper. "This."

She walked around. There was a soiled strip of silver tape on the bottom right side of the bumper.

"I don't know," she said.

He clawed at it with a fingernail, got it loose. It peeled off in a single piece, left shiny chrome beneath it.

He looked up at her. She shrugged.

"First I've seen it," she said. "I don't know where it came from."

He rolled it into a ball.

"Nothing, I guess," he said. "Take care of yourself, Sara. Let me know if there's anything else I can do for you."

"Thanks, Howie."

She helped Danny get belted in, started the engine. Howie waved to them from the bay door, the dog at his feet.

" 'Bye, Reno," Danny called out, though the windows were closed.

He was quiet as they headed home. The sun was setting, the air growing cooler, a cold front moving in. Wisps of fog were beginning to rise from the ground. She thought about the empty compartment.

Billy sitting beside her that morning, saying he'd told her everything.

If the guns were in the trunk, what had been in the compartment? They'd gone over the car with a drug dog, gotten no hits, no traces of residue. More guns? Money?

She'd been on the scene minutes after the shooting, Willis's body still warm. If Billy had taken something from the car, he couldn't have gone far with it. Too much of a risk to put it in his cruiser. He'd have hidden it nearby. Tossed it into the cane or the swamp, gone back to get it later.

*You're holding on to your denial with both hands, aren't you? How much more do you need to know?*

From the backseat, "Mom?"

"What, honey?"

"Did you find what you were looking for?"

She turned to him. He held the tyrannosaurus in his lap, didn't look up.

"Yes," she said and looked back at the road. "I guess I did."

She was getting ready for bed when the phone rang. Barefoot in sweats, she went into the kitchen, picked up the cordless on the second ring, took it into the living room.

"Hello?"

Silence, then a woman's voice.

"You know who this is, right?"

Sara gave that a moment.

"Yes. I think so."

"I'm not even sure why I'm doing this, but I guess I was thinking about that little boy you have. He didn't have anything to do with any of this."

"No, he didn't."

"There's some things going on . . . it's not the way I wanted it, but it might be too late to stop it."

"What —"

"Those people, they don't care about Derek, about me, or about our boys. They're down there for their own reasons."

"I'm not sure I understand."

"You don't need to. I'm just telling you, look out for yourself. And for that little one, too."

"What do you mean?"

There was no answer. Just a click and hiss, and the line was dead.

# TWENTY-TWO

Morgan moved through the woods in the dark. He pushed branches aside, stepped over fallen logs. Soon he could see the lights of the house below. He reached the edge of the trees, looked out across the dead cornfield.

The Camaro and truck were both in the carport, the Camaro's trunk open. Figures moved past the lighted windows of the house.

The cornfield was a dark mass below him. He'd have to make his way through it, try to come up on the house from behind. And stay quiet while he was doing it, try not to break an ankle in a hole, or step into a nest of snakes.

He was halfway down the slope when the front door opened. Flynn looked out, scanned the yard, then disappeared back inside. When he came out again, he was carrying a suitcase and a long-barreled revolver.

He walked to the Camaro, eyes on the yard, the cornfield. He set the suitcase in the trunk, went back in.

A few minutes later, he came out with a smaller case. He put it in the trunk, shut the lid, looked around, the gun still in his hand. Went back inside. Morgan waited.

Five minutes later, Flynn and the woman came out together. They spoke briefly, and she got behind the wheel of the Camaro. Flynn stepped away, looked down the driveway, then cut his eyes back to the cornfield, the woods beyond. His gaze seemed to pass over Morgan, move on.

She started the engine, headlights flashing on, illuminating the truck. Flynn watched as she swung the Camaro around, pointed it back down the driveway, the exhaust rumbling loud.

Morgan waited for Flynn to go inside, then walked back through the woods to the car.

Wisps of fog gathered in the Toyota's headlights, grew thicker as he drove. The night air was cooling. Far ahead he could see the Camaro's taillights, the glitter of the reflecting tape on the bumper.

They were on the county road, heading away from town, little traffic in either direction. He slowed to keep distance between them. The Beretta was on the passenger seat, beneath the half-folded road map.

Ahead on the right was an empty drive-in theater, the screen white and torn, the speaker poles beheaded. He'd passed it on the way here. Now, as he watched, a car came from behind the darkened cashier's shack and bumped onto the road, lights off. It sped after the Camaro.

Morgan killed his own lights, gave the Toyota gas. Gradually he closed the distance. As he got closer, he saw it was a brown Volvo, wondered if it was the same car he'd seen at Delva's. It settled in behind the Camaro by several car lengths, not speeding up or trying to pass.

He floored the gas pedal, powered down the passenger window. The rear of the Volvo loomed large in front of him. Feet from the bumper, he hit the headlights, then the high beams. The inside of the Volvo was flooded with light. Five dark faces turned toward him. Two in the front, three in the back. Dreads, bandanas.

He jerked the Toyota into the left lane, raised the Beretta one-handed, fired twice through the open window, the gun jumping with the recoil. He heard glass explode, and the Volvo swerved away, brakes screeching.

It angled hard onto the shoulder, kicking up dirt, facing back the way it had come.

Morgan set the gun on the seat, gripped the wheel with both hands. He pulled back into the right lane and came up fast on the Camaro's tail. In the glare of his high beams, he could see the woman's face looking back at him in the rearview.

The Camaro leaped ahead with a throaty roar. He stayed on it, the road curving so she had to slow. They came to a bend, and he clenched the wheel, felt it vibrate, heard the Camaro's tires squeal. Then they were back on a straightaway, trees disappearing, open fields on both sides, the Camaro starting to pull away again.

Ahead of them, another bend. He saw the fence where the road curved, the red reflectors on the railings. He started to brake, the wheels drifting, saw the Camaro's headlights illuminate the fence.

The Camaro's brakes screamed as it left the road. It hit the fence broadside, crashed through in a cloud of wood splinters and dust. It spun out in the dirt beyond, headlights tracking across the field, then pointing up at the sky as they came to rest. Dust and smoke swirled in their light.

He steered the Toyota onto the shoulder, dust drifting in his high beams. He picked up the Beretta, got out of the car.

The Camaro had left a ragged gap in the fence, coming to rest about twenty feet into the field, rear tires half-buried in the trenches they'd dug.

Fog crawled along the ground. He looked back down the road. No sign of the Volvo. He stepped into the field.

The Camaro had stalled out, its engine ticking as it cooled. The interior was dark, the back window partially covered with loose dirt. He raised the Beretta in a two-handed grip, stepped over torn-up mounds of earth. He looked down, saw clumps of strawberries.

The windshield was cracked, blood on the inside of the glass. The driver's side window was open. He pointed the Beretta at it as he came around. The woman looked out at him, eyes unfocused. There was a deep cut over her right eye. Her braids were streaked with blood. Her top lip was split.

He moved closer, looked in. Her left leg was bent at an angle under the dashboard. No seat belt. She had a cell phone open, fumbling with it, numbly punching numbers. He reached in with a gloved hand, took it from her. Only two digits on the screen, bloody fingerprints on the keypad.

He closed the phone and dropped it in his pocket.

When he looked back, she was pointing a small automatic at him, the muzzle wavering. He put a hand over it, tugged it from her grip, tossed it behind him.

"You fuckers," she slurred. "You bastards."

He reached in, and she batted weakly at his hand. He switched the ignition off, pulled the keys out. She looked at him, no fear in her eyes.

"You didn't have to do him like that. You didn't."

He went around to the trunk, found the key to open it. He looked back down the highway, then put the Beretta in his waistband, opened the suitcases in turn, and dumped them out into the trunk. Clothes, cosmetics, a small photo album. A teak box of cheap jewelry. In the larger suitcase was a Lady Colt .38, a box of ammunition.

He turned the bags upside-down, shook them. Felt for false bottoms. He pulled up the spare, looked beneath it. Nothing. He shut the trunk.

When he went back to the window, her head was resting on the steering wheel, her breathing shallow. There were bubbles of blood on her lips. He looked into the rear seat. It was empty.

Headlights far down the road, growing brighter, the car coming slow.

He looked at the woman again, thought about nubbed fingers, bloody pruning shears, dominoes.

He knelt, found the automatic, blew dirt from it, worked the slide to chamber a shell. He touched her shoulder through the window.

"Wake up," he said.

She coughed, shook. He dropped the gun in her lap.

"You may need this."

He walked back to the Toyota, got in, killed the lights. When he pulled off the shoulder, the tires fought for traction for a moment, then gained the blacktop. A quarter mile down the road, he looked in his rearview and saw foggy headlight beams illuminate the breach in the fence, the silhouette of a vehicle coming to a stop.

Another quarter mile and he put the lights on. From far back in the distance, he heard faint noises, wondered if they were gunshots.

The Beretta in his lap, he turned into the unpaved driveway, driving slow, lights off. He pulled up into the yard, looked at the house. A light burned over the front steps, but nothing was on inside. The truck was gone.

He got out and went around to the back of the house, the gun at his side. Fog hung over the dead cornfield. No sounds from the house.

The back door gave way on the third kick. He went in with the Beretta up, muzzle pointing into darkness and silence.

He went from room to room. In the bedroom, he turned the light on, saw an open closet door. Clear spaces in the dust where suitcases had been.

In the kitchen, he opened cabinets. Circles in shelf dust, cans missing. The refrigerator empty except for a carton of milk, a bottle of ketchup. A cracked mason jar of preserves lay on the linoleum, contents leaking. No ants yet.

He went back to the Toyota, took the cell phone out, wiped at the blood, pushed buttons until he found the contact list, clicked down, and found BILLY. One entry marked HOUSE, another CELL. He selected it, pushed SEND.

It buzzed three times and then the line opened, faint hissing. Morgan didn't speak.

"Lee-Anne?"

"No," Morgan said.

More silence.

"What did you do to her?"

"You need to talk to your Haitian friends about that."

"Where is she?"

Morgan didn't answer.

"What do you want?"

"Same thing everybody wants. Only difference is, I don't care about you. You can walk away, don't make any difference to me. These others, though, you won't have that luxury."

"So I give it to you and I walk away?"

"That's right. You really think you were going to get to keep it all? That it belonged to you?"

"I need it. To get clear."

"You need some of it. You take ten grand out, leave the rest, tell me where to meet you. Then I'm gone and you can do whatever you want."

"Why should I trust you?"

"Way I look at it, you don't have any choice."

Breathing on the line.

"I need to think on this."

"Nothing to think about," Morgan said. "You give it up, you walk. You don't, you go down, one way or another."

"I need time."

"You got two hours. If I don't hear from

you, I start looking. And I won't be the only one."

He left the Toyota by the barn, used a rag to wipe down anything he might have touched without gloves. In the Monte Carlo, he took his own cell out. Midnight and no missed calls. Nothing from the twins.

He gassed up at an all-night station, went inside, and asked for a phone directory. There was only one Holiday Inn in the county. The attendant gave him directions.

Fifteen minutes later, he was cruising slow past a row of parked cars outside the motel. No Range Rover. He parked, took out his cell, punched in the number he'd gotten from the directory. When the night clerk answered, he asked for Dante Coleman's room. The clerk put him through. They'd used their real names, as he'd guessed.

The line rang a dozen times. The clerk came back on and asked to take a message. Morgan ended the call.

They hadn't wasted any time. They were out there already, looking for the money. His money.

He pulled out of the lot, headed back toward Hopedale. Wondering how much information they had, where they would start.

He needed to calm himself, to think. He turned the stereo on, pushed in the Sam Cooke tape. "Keep Movin' On" came from the speakers.

On the seat beside him, the blood-smeared cell phone began to ring.

# TWENTY-THREE

Fog was settling in as Sara drove the two miles to JoBeth's house. It hung thick over the road, reflecting her headlights back. She turned the wipers and defrosters on. She thought about what Simone James had said.

*It's not the way I wanted it, but it might be too late to stop it.*

Danny stirred in the booster seat, still asleep. She'd taken him from the house in pajamas with a change of clothes in his knapsack, along with the tyrannosaurus. She'd called JoBeth and then dressed quickly, jeans and boots and sweatshirt. The Glock was in her waistpack.

There were headlights behind her now, several car lengths back. She watched them in the rearview. As she neared the turn for JoBeth's street she signaled, slowed. The headlights swung into the left lane and pulled ahead. An SUV jeep of some kind. Its taillights vanished in the fog.

When she pulled into JoBeth's driveway, all the lights were on in the house. Danny stirred again.

"Come on, honey," she said. She swiveled, got him unbelted.

He rubbed sleep from his eyes. "Where are we?"

"JoBeth's."

"Why?"

"You're staying here, little guy, for tonight at least. Come on."

He wrapped his arms around her neck, and she maneuvered him into the front seat with her and opened the door.

"It's foggy," he said. "I'm scared."

"It's okay. There's nothing out there."

She grabbed the knapsack with her free hand, shut the door. As she started up the slate path, the front door opened. JoBeth stood there with her father. He held the door for her as she carried Danny in.

"Thanks, Andy," she said. He wore a bathrobe over pajamas, slippers. He still had the erect posture and flattop haircut of the state highway patrolman he'd once been.

JoBeth reached for Danny. Sara handed him over.

"Sorry to call so late," she said. "I appreciate this."

Danny laid his head on JoBeth's shoulder

and closed his eyes again. She carried him down a hall into a bedroom.

Andy took the knapsack. "Is everything okay, Sara?"

"It might be nothing. I got a phone call that bothered me."

"From who?"

"I'm not positive. But I need to go back to the SO for a while, and I'd feel better if I knew Danny was somewhere safe."

"Back to the office? It's after midnight."

"I know. I may ask you to keep him tomorrow night, too, if that's okay."

"Of course. But you're worrying me."

"Don't be worried. And thanks. I'll call to check in later, if that's okay. I'd feel better."

"Sure, Sara, whatever. He can stay here as long as need be. You, too, if you want."

"Thanks, I'll be okay," she said. She took a last look down the hall where JoBeth and Danny had disappeared. Then she went back out into the fog.

On Cypress Creek Road the fog was so thick she had to slow to thirty-five. The metallic smell of it filled the Blazer, even with the windows up tight. Trees were ghostly shapes by the side of the road, moss-covered branches reaching out. She was glad Danny wasn't with her.

She got her cell out, flipped it open, took her eyes off the road long enough to scroll down to the sheriff's home number. She put her thumb on the SEND button for the second time that day.

*One call and it's over.*

The road began to curve, the white line vanishing in the fog. She felt the right-hand tires bump on the shoulder and she corrected, nervous now, the visibility worse. The wipers clicked, swept moisture from the windshield.

When the road straightened, she looked at the phone again, found Billy's cell number.

*Last chance, Billy. Tell me what's going on.*

She pressed SEND, listened to it ring. Five times and then his voice mail kicked in.

"It's Sara. You need to call me. And you need to do it right away."

She hit END, closed the phone, and put it on the seat beside her. If she didn't hear from him by the time she reached the SO, her next call would be to the sheriff. It would be his decision what to do next. Then it would be out of her hands.

Ahead, a glow in the fog, the fast blink of hazard lights. She slowed, saw the shape of a vehicle, not moving, slewed half onto the shoulder, half on the road, its rear end in the right lane. Headlights pointed out into the woods.

She could guess what had happened. They'd been going too fast and skidded on the wet road, or veered to avoid a deer or some other animal that had popped out of the fog in front of them. Any faster and they would have ended up in the trees.

She let the Blazer coast to a stop on the shoulder and switched her high beams on. It was the vehicle that had passed her earlier. The windows were tinted dark, so she couldn't see inside. She got the emergency light from under the seat, stuck it to the dashboard, plugged it in, and hit the switch. It began to strobe red and blue, flashing off the side of the vehicle ahead, coloring the fog.

She opened her cell and called the main number for the SO.

"St. Charles County Sheriff's."

"Angie, it's Sara Cross. I'm out on Cypress Creek, about . . . a mile north of the Artesia turnoff. There's a vehicle out here, looks like it spun off the road."

"Any injuries?"

"Don't know yet. Can't see anyone. Better send a wrecker, too, get this thing out of the road before someone hits it. It's blocking a lane."

"Tag number?"

"Can't tell from here. I'm going to go out and have a look. Send a unit out, will you? I'll call back if I need an ambo."

"Everyone's pretty busy out there tonight, with this fog and all. Lots of accidents."

"I know that."

"Not sure how quick I can get someone out to your ten-twenty."

Sara breathed out. "Just send someone as soon as you can." *And drop the attitude.*

"Where was that again?"

"Cypress Creek Road, north of Artesia. I've got my emergency flasher on. They can't miss me."

She ended the call, set the phone on the dash, cracked the door. Still no movement in the vehicle. She wondered if they'd walked on to look for help, gotten lost in the fog.

She switched her hazards on and got the spare Maglite from the glove box. When she stepped out onto the road, she adjusted the waistpack so the breakaway tab was in easy reach.

"Sheriff's deputy," she called. "Is anybody hurt?"

No response. The only sound was the slow swish of her wipers, the ticking of the hazards. She thumbed the Maglite button, sending the beam out into the fog. It played along the side of the vehicle, over the tinted windows. The air was heavy, the metallic smell of the fog mixing with the underscent of swamp. The vehicle's hazards pulsed yellow, lit the wet blacktop.

"Hello? Sheriff's deputy. Is there anyone in that vehicle?"

Silence. She considered getting back in the Blazer, waiting for the unit to arrive. Wondered if Angie would put the call out right away or leave her to sweat here for awhile.

*Somebody might be hurt over there. You can't just wait.*

With the Maglite in her left hand, she circled the vehicle, giving it a wide berth. It was a Range Rover, late model from the looks of it. She shone the light on the rear bumper, saw the New Jersey plates, and then a shape came from behind her, silent in the fog. She saw the gun, heard the hammer click back. Cold metal touched her behind the left ear.

"Go ahead and make a move," a low voice said. "You'll die right here."

# Twenty-Four

She froze. The steady click of the hazards seemed to grow louder.

*Stupid. How did I let this happen?*

"Put your hands on that window." The voice a rough whisper.

She thought about turning the Maglite to blind him, pulling at the tab until the Glock was in her hand.

The muzzle touched the base of her skull.

"I'll do you right now. I don't give a fuck."

The driver's door opened, and another man got out. He wore a denim jacket over a hooded sweatshirt, his face in shadow. She wondered if one of them had been the driver of the gray Toyota.

The one behind her reached around and slapped the Maglite from her hand. It hit the blacktop, went out. He pushed her into the side of the Range Rover, pressing on the gun so her cheek touched window glass. His other hand came around, brushed across her stomach and down to the waistpack. He found the buckle and tugged at it until the weight fell away from her. It thunked on the ground.

The gun left her head.

"Open the door." His voice husky as if from a throat injury.

*Remember that detail. Remember everything.*

"I'm not getting in there."

The muzzle again, at the nape of her neck.

"I'm not," she said.

"No? Then maybe we'll go back to where you dropped that boy off. Do our talking there. Your choice."

She closed her eyes. *Don't panic. Think.*

"We need to hurry up," the driver said.

"I called it in when I saw your vehicle," she said. "There'll be deputies here any minute."

"Not soon enough for you."

He caught the collar of her sweatshirt, pulled her away, and kicked her left leg out from under her. She went down onto her side, grunting with the impact, her leg twisted beneath her.

"DeWayne, what the fuck?" the driver said.

Silence. Then the man behind her said "You stupid, you know that?" and she knew he was talking to the driver. Now they would kill her for sure.

"Get up." He hauled up on her sweatshirt and she stood, her left leg threatening to buckle under her. He pulled at the door latch until it opened, the interior light showing a bench seat within, tan leather upholstery. He pushed her in.

"Get down on the floor," he said. Then to the driver, "Get her ride. Pull it off the road. Kill those lights."

"Why?"

"Can't leave it sitting out there. Just do it."

DeWayne crowded in behind her, pushed her down. The muzzle returned to the back of her skull. He pulled the door shut behind him.

"Be cool. We just want to holler at you a little. Don't do nothing stupid, make me put one in your dome."

She heard the Blazer back up, crunch against tree branches. The headlights and emergency flashers went off, the inside of the Range Rover going dark.

She lay with her right cheek pressed into the carpet, DeWayne's weight on her. Her left leg throbbed.

*Pain is good. Pain means you're alive.*

The driver got behind the wheel.

"We need to get out of here, man," he said.

He started the engine, shut the hazards off, backed up into the road.

DeWayne took the gun from her head.

"Just stay there," he said. "Nothing gonna happen to you."

He reached into the front, pressed a switch that reclined the passenger seat enough that he could squeeze past her and into it. She looked up at him for the first time. He was half-turned to face her, a chromed automatic in his left hand, her waistpack in his lap. He wore a hooded black sweatshirt, had a lazy left eye.

*Another detail. Remember it.*

He pushed the hood back, looked down at her. He was heavier than the driver, but there was a similarity in their features.

"Where we going?" the driver said. "Where we taking her?"

"Just drive. We'll do our talking right here."

She tried to sit up.

"Stay down there," DeWayne said. "We cool like this."

They picked up speed. She wondered how long Angie had waited to put the call out, if there was a cruiser behind them somewhere now.

*Too late.*

DeWayne pulled the tab on the waistpack. The front flap fell away, exposing the Glock.

"Check this shit out," he said. He tugged it free. "Sweet."

He opened the big glove box, put the Glock inside, shut it.

"We gonna make this brief," he said to her. "Where it at?" He moved the gun to his right hand.

"I don't know what you —" she said, and he leaned forward and slapped her hard in the face. It snapped her head to the side, stung her cheek. Tears came to her eyes.

"Gonna be a long night, you keep that shit up," he said.

"We should go back to her house," the driver said. "Nobody there now."

"Nah," DeWayne said. "They find her car, they might go there looking for her. We cool where we are."

"I don't like this fog, man. I can't see shit."

"Just take it slow. We be all right." He looked back at her. "I'll say it again. Where it at?"

"I don't understand." The fear strong inside her now. They wanted something she couldn't give them. When they realized that, she'd be no more use to them.

"What, your boyfriend cut you out of the deal? Didn't give you a slice of that nice pie? Three hundred and fifty gees. Should be enough to go around. He keep all that shit himself?"

*Three hundred and fifty thousand.*

She thought about the empty compartment in the Honda.

*Oh Christ, Billy, what did you do?*

The Blazer was gone from the woman's driveway, only one light on in the house. Morgan cruised by slow. No movement inside. If the twins had been here, they were gone.

Flynn had said he'd needed time to get the money, would call tomorrow and name the place. It might be a setup, or maybe he'd realized Morgan was right, that the only way clear of this was to deal.

The only loose end was the twins. Running around out there, muddying the waters. Making things complicated that should have been simple. He headed back toward the county road, the fog thick now, no other cars out. The Range Rover would be hard to miss. If they were out there, he would find them.

"Must be a greedy motherfucker," De-Wayne said. "Leave you out, not even give you a taste."

*Tell him something. Anything. Keep him talking. Play for time.*

"I don't know where the money's at," she said.

"But you know who do, right?"

Wondering how much they knew, how far she could bluff them.

"Maybe. I'm not sure."

"We got all night," he said. "So maybe we go back, get that little one, take him for a ride with us, improve your memory. What you think?"

"That won't help."

"We'll find out."

Headlights in the rearview, far back but moving fast. *Finally.*

"Yo," the driver said.

DeWayne looked out the back window.

"Maybe she was telling the truth," the driver said. "About calling it in."

The headlights grew.

"Slow down," DeWayne said. "If it's just some car, it'll pass. If it's police, he'll try to get up on us. If he does, pull over. I'll take care of it."

"You need to stop this vehicle and let me out," she said. "That's your only chance to get away."

"Quiet, bitch."

The Range Rover slowed. The headlights

held steady behind them.

"I don't like this shit," the driver said.

"Just chill. Watch the road."

The headlights larger.

"DeWayne," the driver said.

Sara looked at the door, the latch in easy reach. If they pulled over, she'd grab for it, try to get out, warn the deputy if she could.

*And get shot in the back maybe. But what other choices are there? Better to take the chance running than stay in here.*

"Be cool," DeWayne said. "If it were police, he would've lit us up already."

Behind them, the car's turn signal blinked.

The driver let out his breath. "It's all right. He's passing."

The car swung out behind them, came abreast, and then pulled ahead fast.

"What's up with that fool?" the driver said.

Then he was standing up on the brakes, the tires screeching. He jerked the wheel to the right, and the momentum threw her forward into the seats. When she looked up, she saw the car had cut them off, swung into their lane. They thumped up onto the shoulder, back onto the road as the driver corrected, then rolled to a stop. The headlights dimmed as the engine sputtered and stalled.

"Mother*fucker*," the driver said.

She could see over the dashboard now. Saw the car ahead of them pull over, almost out of sight, taillights glowing in the fog.

"That motherfucker blind?" the driver said.

"Don't stop," DeWayne said. "Keep going. Pull around him."

She saw a shape coming through the fog. The driver of the other car coming back to see if they were all right. She looked at the doorlatch.

"Just sit right there," DeWayne said to her. "Don't move."

"Motherfucker come back to apologize, I'm gonna beat his ass," the driver said.

"Pull out," DeWayne said.

The driver cranked the ignition, and as the engine fired up she heard a flat crack like a board breaking. The windshield on the driver's side starred. His head snapped back, and something wet and warm spattered her face.

DeWayne made no sound. He popped the door open, slid out. More shots, glass imploding. She ducked down, saw the driver slumped over the wheel, blood all over the seatback. She lunged across the console and passenger seat, staying low, and got the glove box open, her hand on the Glock.

■ ■ ■ ■

Morgan put the first shot through the Range Rover's windshield, saw it hit, and then the passenger door was open, DeWayne moving fast. Morgan steadied the Beretta with both hands, tracked him, fired three times. The first shot blew out the door window, the second went high, and the third caught him in the hip, spun him but didn't drop him. Morgan heard him grunt in pain, and then he was away from the Range Rover and gone in the fog.

Morgan moved out of the headlights, put two shots through the grille, steam hissing out. The engine coughed and died. He looked into the fog-shrouded woods, waiting for DeWayne to show himself. Then the Range Rover's left rear door opened, and someone spilled out. He swiveled to take aim, saw it was the woman deputy. She hit the ground and came up fast, using the door for cover, a gun in her hand.

He backed away into the fog.

Sara moved to the rear of the Range Rover, trying to get it between her and whoever else was out there. It had come to rest at an angle, front tires in the right lane, rear still on the shoulder. She crouched, listening. To her right, where DeWayne had gone, a solid wall of fog, the phantom shapes of trees. She heard something move there, a dragging footstep.

She raised up, but the tint on the rear windows was too dark to see through. To see ahead she'd have to look around the corner of the Range Rover, expose herself. She thought of her cell phone, left on the Blazer's dashboard. *How stupid was that?*

More noises from the trees. She'd heard DeWayne cry out, guessed he was hit, but had no idea how bad. The driver had taken a head shot. He was out of the play. But where was the other shooter?

*Stay calm. Watch, listen, and think. Survive this.*

"Yo, Morgan," DeWayne called. "You hear me, man?"

The voice off to her right, hard to tell how far. Then more dragging footsteps, closer to the Range Rover. He was being smart, moving away from where he'd called out.

No answer from the fog.

"Cops be here any minute," DeWayne said. "It don't have to play out like this. Just be on your way." More movement.

She gripped the Glock with both hands, looked around the left rear corner, saw the taillights ahead in the fog. The shooter's car. She pulled back.

*You've got cover. Stay there. Don't take any chances. Think about Danny.*

A slight thump against the right side of the Range Rover. DeWayne using it for cover.

No sound. The fog seemed to close in around her.

"Yo, Morgan, we know where the money at, man. Let's talk this out."

If DeWayne was moving toward the back of the Range Rover, he'd find her. Or worse, she'd end up in the field of fire between him and the other shooter, wherever he was.

"Police!" she called out. "Drop your weapons! Both of you!"

Silence.

"Sheriff's Office! Units are on their way. Put your weapons down."

A faint sound to her left. DeWayne's breathing, low but labored. Closer now, maybe four feet away. She could wait for him to find her, or she could swing around, get her weapon on him, hope she was faster.

She thought of Danny, sleeping soundly, trusting her to be there when he woke up. To tell him everything was okay.

The breathing inched closer. She gripped the Glock tighter, finger on the trigger. Now was the time.

*Danny, forgive me.*

She turned the corner, gun out, arms extended, yelled, "Police!" and DeWayne was right there, closer than she'd thought, and he caught the barrel of the Glock and wrenched it to the side, his own gun at her face. She threw herself to the left, saw the muzzle flash, felt the heat, knew he'd missed. He hammered a shoulder into her, his weight behind it, and as she hit the side of the Range Rover he twisted the Glock out of her hands. She lunged for it, missed, caught a knee that knocked her back onto the blacktop.

He stepped back, tossed the Glock away, pointed his gun down at her. She saw his finger tighten on the trigger, heard the *crack* of the shot and then pink mist filled the air. He fell away from her, onto his side, and lay still.

A figure came out of the fog behind him. A tall black man, gray hair, wearing a dark windbreaker, pointing an automatic at her.

She rolled onto her knees, struggling to breathe. She saw where the Glock lay a few feet away on the shoulder, knew she'd never reach it.

"I'm a sheriff's deputy," she said.

"I know."

She looked up at him. Got one foot under her, then another. She rose shakily, her back to the Range Rover, breathing heavy. If he was going to shoot her, he'd have to do it like this, standing. Not on her knees.

The muzzle of the gun followed her up, steadied, maybe three feet from her forehead. Gloved finger on the trigger.

*Danny.*

"I don't have the money," she said. Her chest rose and fell.

"I know."

"I don't know anything about it."

"Doesn't matter now."

She closed her eyes, wondered if she'd hear the shot.

"I have a little boy," she said.

"I know."

She looked at him then, met his eyes.

He lowered the gun.

As she watched, he stepped back, picked up her Glock, and tossed it into the woods. He looked at her for a moment, then turned and walked away into the fog.

She knelt by DeWayne, trying not to look at what was left of his face. Felt beneath him until her fingers touched metal. With a heave, she rolled him off the chromed automatic, picked it up, slick with his blood. She worked the slide to make sure a round was chambered, moved fast to the front of the Range Rover. The man was only a silhouette in the fog now, walking toward his car. She aimed.

"Stop right there!"

He did.

"Turn around slow and drop your weapon."

He didn't move.

"You going to shoot me in the back?" he said.

The gun was unsteady in her hands. She tightened her grip, set the front sight on him. "Just put your weapon down."

After a moment, he said, "I didn't think so," and walked on, the fog closing in around him.

She watched him go, her finger slackening on the trigger.

*Whoever he is, he just saved your life.*

She heard a car door shut, the hiss of tires. Watched the glow of the taillights fade.

She listened until she couldn't hear anything else, then lowered the gun. She stood alone in the fog and silence.

Morgan kept it to thirty-five on the drive back to the motel, watching the rearview, the still-warm Beretta on his lap.

He doubted she'd gotten a good look at

the car or plates. DeWayne had used his name, but it wouldn't do her much good. One more day here and he was gone.

He'd get the money from Flynn, do whatever it took to make that happen. But he couldn't go back to Newark now. He'd call Cassandra from someplace safe, have her and the boy meet him. He'd have to find a way to get to the bank, empty his safe deposit. Then head west maybe, keep driving.

He thought about the woman deputy. Remembered her carrying her little boy in the park, hitched up on her shoulders. Tonight she'd gone head-to-head with DeWayne rather than run and hide in the fog. Had stood and looked Morgan in the eye as he held the Beretta on her, his finger on the trigger. He'd seen the fear there, but something else beyond it. Something that was stronger.

The fog was starting to break up, the road clearing in his headlights. He turned the stereo back on, pushed the tape in. Sam Cooke wishing someone would come and ease his troublin' mind.

One more day and gone.

# Twenty-Five

Four A.M., and the Sheriff's Office was abuzz. Off-duty deputies had shown up as the news got out. Sara sat slumped in the chair facing the sheriff's desk, her right ear still echoing with the shot DeWayne had fired. She ached all over, and the adrenaline aftershock was starting to fade, a stonelike fatigue taking its place.

She could see the sheriff and Sam Elwood talking by the dispatcher's desk, Sam with his hands on his hips. He turned, met her eyes.

She stretched her legs, rubbed her calf where DeWayne had kicked her. Outside, she could see thin fog drifting past the floodlights, stars starting to appear in the sky.

The sheriff came back in carrying a manila folder and a bottle of water. He cracked the cap, handed it to her.

"Thanks."

He closed the door and settled behind his desk. "How do you feel?"

"Tired," she said.

"I can imagine."

"I just want to see Danny."

"You will. I talked to Andy Ryan a few minutes ago. Everything's fine. I sent a deputy out there as well."

She took a long drink of water.

He opened the folder, took out a black-and-white photo on printer paper, and set it in front of her.

"New Jersey State Police sent that down. Look familiar?"

She pulled the photo closer. It was the man DeWayne had called Morgan.

"That's him," she said. "He's younger here, though. Man I saw was in his fifties, sixties maybe. Like he'd been around."

"He has. That photo's a few years old. Name's Nathaniel Morgan. Fifty-seven, kind of old for this sort of thing. He has a jacket going back to the sixties — assault, attempted murder, manslaughter. Did seven years on the last one, 1980 to '87."

"Who were the other two?"

He read from the file.

"Dante and DeWayne Coleman. Brothers. Both have substantial sheets. DeWayne, the big one, just got out of state prison two months ago, for aggravated assault. A couple of princes, those two."

"Have you found Billy?"

He sat back. "Sam just came back from his place. He's gone, of course. I left Minos McCarthy and Ed Strunk out there in a cruiser, see if he comes back. I'm doubting he will. Looks like he packed up, hit the road. Any idea where he might have gone?"

She shook her head. "I tried his cell a half-dozen times," she said. "It's turned off. I think he's got a brother in Ocala —"

"We know. I put in a call to the Marion County SO up there. They're out at the house now. No sign of him, and the brother says he hasn't seen or heard from him in weeks. No, I'm thinking it's somewhere nearby, somewhere he thinks is safe. A fishing camp or a hunting cabin or something."

"If he has one, he never told me."

"On the other hand, if all this is true, he can go a long way on three hundred and fifty thousand dollars."

All of it was catching up with her now, hearing someone else speak it. The signs she should have seen. The things that were in front of her all along she never put together, didn't want to put together.

*Now here you are. What good did you do after all?*

"We put a BOLO out on the truck," he said. "Unless he's got another vehicle stashed somewhere, we'll find him soon. My guess is he's holed up somewhere close, especially if he's carrying that money around."

"Maybe he isn't. Maybe Lee-Anne has it."

"If she did, someone took it from her."

"What do you mean?"

"Call came in about an hour ago. FHP found her car abandoned down in Hendry County. Gone off the road, all busted up. Blood on the seat."

"And?"

"They alerted the Sheriff's Office down there. Tracks show there were a couple other cars at the scene. They're trying to chase it down. She had suitcases in the trunk, but someone had been through them. From the amount of blood, the condition of the car, unlikely she walked away."

"Someone took her."

"Looks like. And not to a hospital. This thing's sprawling, Sara, and bad. FDLE's out at your scene. Tampa FBI's been notified as well. This whole thing gets taken away from us in twenty-four hours, I'm guessing. Unless we find Billy first."

"Can you GPS his phone?"

"No luck so far. Either he shut it down or

figured out how to deactivate the tracking applet. If he uses it again, we might get lucky. Until then . . ."

He tapped an unsharpened pencil on the desk.

"Elwood's got your service weapon," he said. "He'll give it to you before you leave. You'll need to clean it good, though. Some dirt in the barrel and all."

He touched his left cheek. "You might want to do something about that too."

She raised a hand to her face, felt the stickiness there. He took a tissue from the box next to his terminal, handed it over. She folded it, dabbed it with water from the bottle, wiped her cheek. It came away red.

"You handled yourself well out there," he said.

"How's that?" She dabbed water, wiped again. More blood. "I had my service weapon taken away from me. Twice."

"You came back in one piece. That's the main thing."

"I guess."

"Maybe this Morgan did you a favor, taking those two out like that. Kept you from having to make that choice. It's not an easy thing, shooting a man. It can be tough to live with. You can give it all the context and justification you want, but it still goes against human nature. I haven't fired a shot in anger since the war, and that's the way I want to keep it."

She looked at the bloody tissue.

"That's one of the things I can't get my head around," he said. "Billy shooting that boy that way. What makes a good man — a good deputy — do something like that?"

"Money."

"Did he really think he was going to get away with it? That much money? That someone wasn't going to come looking for it?"

"I don't know. Maybe he was tired of the way things were. Maybe he saw this as his chance."

"His chance to get killed."

"Maybe he thought he could handle it, handle whatever came after, too."

He tapped the pencil.

"Would have thought he was smarter than that. But money can do that to a person, I guess. Wake up one day, think they deserve something they haven't earned. Decide to go out and take it. But it never works out. They can never hold on to it."

"I wouldn't know," she said.

"Money. People think it'll cure all their troubles. Then they find out the way things really work."

"How's that?"

"Forget about money," he said. "Pain's the only currency. And everybody pays their way."

She pulled up the driveway to JoBeth's house. A cruiser was parked in the sideyard, Clay Huff at the wheel, drinking takeout coffee. He nodded at her as she got out, went up the steps. The sky to the east was lightening.

She knocked softly, and Andy Ryan opened the door. He was dressed, a clip-on holster on his belt, a .38 snugged there.

"Come on in, Sara. Are you okay?"

"I'm fine. How's Danny?"

"Still sleeping. He got up once during the night, asked for you, but that's it."

"He know about any of this?"

"No."

"Good."

He shut the door behind her.

"I'll make up my bed for you," he said. "I'm up for the day anyway, already had my first cup of coffee."

"That's okay. I don't want to put you to any trouble."

"No trouble at all."

"I want to check on Danny first."

"Go on."

She went down the hall to the extra bedroom, the door ajar, a night-light on. She opened the door wider, saw him there, sleeping on his side, hugging the pillow against him, breathing softly. Fragile.

It was a teenager's bed, had belonged to JoBeth's brother before her parents divorced and he'd gone to live with his mother in Gainesville. Danny seemed lost in it.

*Someday, sooner than you expect, he'll be a teenager himself, with a life beyond the hospital and doctors and drugs. Then an adult, with, please God, all this sickness just a bad memory. Someday he'll leave your house, make his own life. He'll be a man, and you'll be old and gray. And alone.*

She shut the door quietly behind her, sat on a chair, and pulled off her mud-spattered sneakers and socks. Her sweatshirt came next, leaving the T-shirt she wore underneath. She climbed into the bed, her back to the wall, and put an arm around him. He stirred, mumbled.

She laid her head on the pillow, felt him breathing next to her, and slipped into a deep and dreamless sleep.

# TWENTY-SIX

By the next afternoon, the cold front had blown through and gone. Sara drove out to CR-23 in the Blazer, pulled onto the shoulder and parked. The sky was bright blue, dotted with billowy white clouds. Sugarcane moved in the breeze.

Why she'd come here, she wasn't sure. She got out, walked along the edge of the incline. There was no sign of the teddy bear or cross, though she knew she had the right location. She wondered if a roadside trash crew had picked them up.

She took off her sunglasses, hung them from the collar of her sweatshirt, looked around. Swamp on one side, cane fields on the other, the dark shape of the abandoned Highfield refinery in the distance. Billy's father had worked there, his grandfather before him. It had been closed for fifteen years, all those jobs gone south, out of the county, the building left to rot.

The air was cooler now, the sun starting to sink. Her left leg ached, and there was still a faint ringing in her right ear. She went back to the Blazer, sat with the door open, got the Aleve from the glove box, shook two out, washed them down with a long swig from a bottle of water. She looked back at the refinery, already deepening in shadow.

She hung her sunglasses on the rearview, got her cell phone from the waistpack, called JoBeth.

"How are you making out?" Sara said.

"Fine, we're watching TV. I was about to start making dinner. Are hot dogs all right?"

"Sure, Danny loves them. Is there a deputy there still?"

"Yes. They changed shifts again. Should I bring something out to him?"

"Not a bad idea."

"When will you be back?"

"Twenty minutes, half hour at the most." She looked at the darkening refinery. "But if Danny's hungry, go ahead and start without me."

"You sure?"

"Yeah, that's fine. I'll call you on my way back."

*Maybe it's worth checking out. Have a look, scratch it off the list.*

If she called the sheriff, he'd scramble a

tactical team double time, maybe twenty men, half a dozen vehicles. Bring them all the way out here so she could sheepishly explain why she'd called in the cavalry for no good reason. Why she hadn't bothered to check it out herself first, had sat in the car until the men arrived. And if there was nothing there, it would all be a waste. Worse than a waste.

*You're a sheriff's deputy. You're out here now. It'll take five minutes. Have a look, head back.*

She shut the phone, dropped it on the passenger seat, started the engine.

As it grew dark, Morgan packed the last of his things in the Monte Carlo, checked the room again. He wouldn't be coming back.

He sat on the bed, ejected the Beretta clip, reloaded it, slid it back home. He checked the Walther as well, chambered a round, lowered the hammer.

Flynn had called that afternoon, given him a time and place. If it was a setup, Morgan would be ready for him. If the money wasn't there, he would make Flynn take him where it was. End it there and be on the road by midnight, heading north.

He slid his right pants leg up, exposing the elastic ankle support he'd bought at a drugstore that day. The Walther went into it, tight against the skin, but easily reached. He let the pants leg drop down to cover it.

When he stood, the pain hit him with such suddenness it took his breath away. He stumbled into the bathroom, barely got his pants down before it came, a hot rush that seemed to flush out his entire body. Sweat filmed his forehead. He wiped at it. It was thick, oily, and harsh.

He sat on the toilet until the cramps stopped and his muscles started to relax. When he could move again, he cleaned off, flushed. He drank from the faucet, splashed more water on his face. He thought about the Vicodin, decided against it. He would need to be sharp. The pain would be better. It would keep him focused.

After a while, he left the bathroom, shut out the light. He pulled on the windbreaker and gloves, used a hand towel to wipe down everything he might have touched. Then he got the Beretta from the bed and left the room for the last time.

Sara turned down the refinery service road, the Blazer rumbling over the metal bridge that spanned the canal. The refinery was three stories high, set back from the road. Weathered wood, broken windows, gaping holes in the sloped roof. She drove slow, the road pitted and worn.

There was a chain-link fence around the property, sagging in spots. A metal frame gate with steel letters — *HF* — mounted on it, like the brand from a western ranch. Beyond the gate was what would have been the truck yard, a hard dirt clearing surrounded by overgrown brush and scrub trees. The road continued past, up to some small satellite buildings, shacks really, low and empty, windows boarded. Workers' quarters maybe. The paint all but stripped from them by wind and weather.

She parked the Blazer, got out. The gate was secured by loops of chain, a heavy padlock. The lock was rusted shut, its coating of grit and dust undisturbed.

She got back in the Blazer, drove up the road toward the shacks, parked in front of them, shut the engine off. As she stepped out onto the hard ground, she tugged the Velcro snap of the waistpack, closed her hand on the Glock, drew it out, and held it at her side.

Three shacks, side by side, the plywood on the windows still tight. The doors had been nailed shut with sawn boards. She tugged at them, no give.

She went around to the back. No windows

on this side. There was a small tractor barn farther back, sliding door pulled shut. She looked at the ground, saw no tracks of any kind, as if the dirt had been brushed clean.

Nearly dark now. She went to the barn and pushed at the door. It creaked, slid open a foot. The glint of metal inside, the silver of a high bumper. A truck.

From behind her, Billy said, "Hey, Sara."

She didn't move. Her hand tightened on the Glock.

"You shouldn't have come here," he said.

She tried to swallow, couldn't.

"The sheriff's on his way," she said.

"I don't think so. If he was, you would have waited for him, right? Or maybe not, way you are. Doesn't matter now, though. Go ahead and turn around. Not too fast, though, okay?"

She turned, saw the gun. It was a Colt Python .357 with a ventilated barrel. She'd seen him with it before, at the range. He raised it now, pointed it at her face. She didn't move, the Glock still hanging at her side.

They looked at each other. He wore jeans, boots, a flannel shirt, sleeves buttoned. Dark circles under his eyes.

"Should have given you more credit," he said. "Guess I always did underestimate you. Why don't you go ahead and let that weapon drop?"

She shook her head. "Can't do it."

He steadied the gun. She looked into the darkness of the wide muzzle. *Breathe. Think.*

"I've got nothing to lose, Sara. Not anymore."

When she didn't move, he thumbed the Python's hammer back. She heard the drag and click.

"Let it go," he said. "Think about Danny."

She looked from the gun to his eyes. She let her grip loosen. The Glock fell to the dirt.

"Now take a couple steps back," he said. "Stop. That's good."

He came forward, the Colt still on her, dipped and picked up the Glock.

"You wouldn't be carrying a backup weapon, would you?"

"No."

"Why don't you pull up the legs of your jeans there? One at a time."

She did, looking up at him as she bent.

"Okay," he said. "Let's take a walk. Get out in front of me. I'll tell you where to go."

"Why don't you let the hammer on that pistol down?"

"Through those trees there. Go on."

When she came to a gap in the fence, the

chain-link sagging almost to the ground, she said, "I can't see where I'm going. It's too dark."

"You're fine. Just watch going over, some sharp ends there. And please, Sara, don't try to run. I don't want to hurt you, but I will if you make me."

She lifted a leg high enough to clear the hanging fence, stepped over, and brought the other one up behind. She took two steps, stopped, heard him cross the fence behind her.

"To your right."

They passed through trees, thin branches snapping at her in the dark, then came into the clearing behind the refinery. There was a loading dock back here, and a rusted two-story framework that had once been a chute and conveyor system. Across the back wall was a long row of windows, most of them broken.

"Go on," he said. "Through the door."

She saw it then, a metal door, rusted hinges. She hesitated.

"I can't leave you roaming around out here, Sara. Not now. Go on in." She heard him come up behind her.

At the door, she reached out, put a palm against cold metal, pushed. It swung open into blackness.

Morgan almost missed the refinery in the dark. No lights out here, just a canal and cane fields on one side of the road, swamp on the other. When he got to the crossroads and the blinking yellow light, he realized he'd gone too far. He pulled onto the shoulder, backed and filled, killed his lights, and headed back the way he'd come, the road long and straight and empty. He powered the window down, listening.

The moon was low in the sky, but bright enough that he could see the dark outline of the refinery. He slowed, saw the bridge and the access road Flynn had told him about. He drove past.

There was another farther down, as he'd expected. He turned down it, slowing the Monte Carlo to a creep. He bumped over the bridge, heard metal groan, drove slowly ahead into darkness.

# TWENTY-SEVEN

When she stepped through the doorway, she heard Billy come in behind her, the rusted creak of the hinges, a bolt being thrown. He touched her on the back, prodded her forward.

"Go ahead," he said. They were in almost total darkness.

Noises to her right. She turned to see him lighting a Coleman lantern with a match. He set the lamp atop an overturned crate, adjusted the wick until the flame grew brighter. He still held the Python. Her Glock was tucked into his belt.

They were in a big, high-ceilinged room, the concrete floor stained and chipped, the remnants of some type of machinery in one corner. On the front wall, massive sliding doors, closed now, a smaller door beside them. Grids and gaps in the concrete where other equipment had once been, empty crates. An iron staircase led up to a second-floor catwalk. There were gaping holes in the ceiling, and she could see the first stars against the blackness.

"What am I going to do with you, Sara? You always complicate things."

He eased the Python's hammer down, pointed to her waistpack. "Your cell in there?"

She shook her head.

"You sure?"

"It's back in the Blazer."

Something fluttered near the ceiling. She looked up.

"Pigeons," he said. "Bats in here, too. Didn't get more than an hour's sleep all night."

Her eyes were adjusting. There was trash scattered on the floor, broken bottles, graffiti on the walls. A sooty blotch against one wall, as if from a fire.

"Nice place, isn't it?" he said. "Go on up those stairs there."

"Why?"

"Just do it, Sara. We don't have a lot of time."

The stairs were spotted with pigeon droppings, rust. She went up slowly, heard him behind her. He'd left the lamp where it was, but its glow was bright enough that she could see where she was going. Sweat crept down the nape of her neck.

"Up there on the left," he said.

She reached the catwalk, saw the open door there.

"Go on," he said. "I'm right behind you."

She went in, heard the scratching of another match. He lit a thick candle, set it on the floor.

It was a long empty room, stripped of machinery, a tangle of pipes protruding from one wall. The ceiling was pressed tin. There was a single big front window, half the panes missing.

On the concrete floor near the window was a wooden pallet, a sleeping bag stretched out on it. Atop the sleeping bag was a Bushmaster AR-15 and an olive drab duffel bag. There was a small camping stove in the corner, a cardboard box of groceries.

"Over there," he said. "Stay away from the window. Go ahead, sit down."

She lowered herself to the floor, her back to the wall, watching him. To her left was a black nylon gearbag, zippered shut.

He went to the window, looked out.

"I saw you," he said. "From up here. I guess I shouldn't have been surprised. You never did give up easy."

He set the Python on the windowsill, picked up the rifle. He looked out again and then used the butt to bump out the remaining panes of glass.

"I've got the high ground," he said. "That's something, I guess."

He sat on the sleeping bag, his back against the wall, facing her, the window above him, the rifle in his lap.

"I used to come here as a kid," he said. "I ever tell you that?"

"No."

"My father was assistant foreman, until his accident. My mother and I would come here sometimes, bring his lunch. I couldn't wait to get out of here, away from the noise, the dust. Those rollers would be going nonstop, twenty-four seven. You could almost feel that shit in your lungs."

He pulled the candle close to him, ejected the rifle's magazine. She looked at him, at the Python on the sill above him.

"All I could think about was how I never wanted to end up in a place like this."

From the duffel, he took another magazine, a roll of duct tape. A draft came through the window, set the candle flame flickering.

As she watched, he ripped strips from the roll, taped the magazines together, open ends in opposite directions.

"Who are you expecting?" she said.

"Someone. Soon."

He fit the magazine back into the receiver, slapped it into place.

*Easy. Calm. Don't let him know you're scared.*

"Billy, this has all gone too far."

"I guess it has."

"Lee-Anne —"

"I know. He told me."

"Who?"

"One of the men who did it, maybe. I don't know." He worked the bolt, laid the rifle across his lap, rubbed his right sleeve across his forehead. "Christ, it's hot in here."

"This doesn't have to go any further," she said.

"Too late for that. How much you tell Hammond?"

"All of it."

"Too bad."

Moonlight was beginning to filter through the window. He looked at his watch.

"We agreed on an hour from now," he said, "but I imagine he'll be along a good bit before that. Maybe bring some people with him, too."

"What people?"

"Ones that money belonged to, I expect. Or them that want it now. Doesn't matter either way. Didn't know how long I'd need to hide out here. It was almost a relief, getting that call."

She thought about Danny at JoBeth's, eating dinner now maybe, or watching TV, wondering where she was.

*You have to think clearly. You have to get out of this.*

"They're coming here?" she said.

"One of them is, at least. He said he wanted to cut a deal. I told him yes."

"What kind of deal?"

"I keep a little, give him the rest. That's what he told me. Can't imagine that's their plan, though. Anyway, I'm ready for them."

"Billy, this is crazy. We need to get out of here."

"I've already killed one man. What difference does it make I kill a couple more?"

"We can walk out of here right now."

"I can't go to prison, Sara. You know that."

"We can talk to the sheriff."

"You think that's going to do any good? This isn't about any throwdown, Sara. I shot that boy. I told him to walk down into that swamp and turn and face me. And when he did — so scared he was almost pissing himself — I looked him right in the eye and I shot him in the chest. Then I shot him twice more. To be sure."

She said nothing.

"He didn't understand what was going on, even after I shot him the first time. He never knew."

"You're not going to be able to get away, Billy. The only way out of this is to give yourself up."

"You're right about one thing. The people that want that money, they'll keep coming. Even if I did get away, they'd keep chasing me. That's why it's got to end here, tonight, one way or another. It's the only chance I've got."

"This is wrong. This isn't the way to do it."

"I'm sorry you had to be here for this, Sara, but I'm out of options. If they want that money, they're going to have to take it from me."

The patch of moonlight grew on the floor.

"It's not too late," she said. "We can walk out to the Blazer, be gone before they get here. We can call the sheriff. He'll listen to your side of it."

"Always looking out for me, aren't you? Trying to get me to do the right thing, keep me from fucking up. And I never cut you a break, did I? I fought you all the way."

He pointed at the gearbag.

"Go ahead, open it," he said. "See what

all the fuss was."

"I don't want to."

"No, you should. Go ahead. That's what this is all about, right?"

She tugged the bag closer, still watching him.

"Go on."

She worked the zipper slowly, as if the bag were full of snakes. As the edges parted she saw bricks of money inside, wrapped in clear plastic. The top brick was hundreds.

"Hell of a thing, isn't it?" he said. "They make that in a couple days up there. Selling poison to kids."

"That give you the right to take it?"

"It belongs to whoever has it. When I first saw that money, all wrapped up like that, you know what I thought? That's my ticket out. Enough money to start over somewhere else, away from here, get something going. I guess I should have known better."

"It was Lee-Anne, wasn't it? It was her idea."

"Doesn't matter now."

"It'll make a difference to a jury."

"Drop it, Sara." He took a pair of stainless steel handcuffs from the duffel.

"I'm not putting those on," she said.

He tossed them clattering at her feet. "Don't make this harder than it is," he said.

"We don't have much time."

"Go ahead and shoot me now. I'm not doing it."

"You don't mean that."

"Try me."

He set the Bushmaster on the floor, took the Glock from his belt, and put it beside the rifle. In a flash he was on her. She kicked out, but he batted her foot away, dropped his weight onto her. She got the heel of her hand under his jaw, pushed up, her nails scoring his skin, but his left hand locked around her throat, pinned her down, all his weight on it.

Her knees pumped, trying for his groin, thumping into his legs as he changed position. She got her right hand free, made a fist, and swung hard into his temple.

His face was mottled red above her, the veins and muscles standing out in his neck, lips pulled back over his teeth. She could smell him, woodsmoke and sweat and something else beneath it all, sour and vile. Spots were beginning to flash in her peripheral vision. *I'm going to black out.*

"Stop it, Sara. Goddammit . . . stop fighting me."

She hit him again, a short sharp jab to his face, and then his own hand raised up, and she saw the fist coming down, tried to turn away from it.

Her head snapped back and hit the floor, and for a moment waves seemed to pass in front of her, as if she were standing too close to a fire. She let her hands drop, Billy's face swimming before her eyes. Then she felt his weight leave her, something hard cinch across her right wrist and ratchet closed. He dragged her across the floor, her arm stretched from the socket. Then a second ratchet and he was away from her, breathing heavy, retreating to his spot near the wall.

She looked at the ceiling, gulped air. Her face felt swollen and thick.

"God*dammit*, Sara."

The room steadied around her. She touched her face. No blood, but she could already feel the swelling there. She looked to her right, saw he'd locked the loose cuff around an L-shaped bend of copper pipe that came from the wall, ran down into the floor. She pulled at it. It didn't move.

She tried to sit up. He was touching the nail marks on his chin, looking at the blood on his fingertips. He picked up the Glock.

"Easiest thing for me to do is kill you right now," he said. "Smart thing, too. One less loose end. You know that, right? It won't matter much in the long run. At least not to me."

She tasted blood in her mouth, turned her head and spat.

He rose, looked out the window again, silhouetted against the moonlight, brighter now.

"You shouldn't have come alone, Sara," he said without turning. "You shouldn't have come at all."

# Twenty-Eight

A hundred yards up the service road, Morgan stopped, shut the engine off. In the distance, he could see the refinery, moonlight on broken glass, gaps in the roof.

He slipped out of the car, the Beretta in his hand. Separating this road from the refinery was a half mile of choked undergrowth, stunted trees. He heard night noises, animal sounds he couldn't identify. A splashing from the canal behind him, a low bellow in the dark.

As he started up the road, the breeze shifted, brought with it the smell of swamp. Then something else. Cigarette smoke.

He stopped where he was, waited for his eyes to adapt to the dark. There was a shape ahead, a car, someone at the wheel. The glow of a cigarette being drawn on, and then sparks as it sailed from the window, landed in the dirt.

He held his breath. A mosquito landed on

his neck. He didn't touch it.

He counted to ten, then moved closer. It was a dark four-door sedan, a Lexus maybe. He came up silently on the driver's side. The man at the wheel had dreadlocks, a blue bandana around his neck. The woman had talked. The Haitians had beaten him here.

He swung the Beretta through the open window, hit the driver across the bridge of the nose. It snapped his head back, and Morgan hit him again before he could cry out, yanked at the door latch and pulled it open. The man spilled out onto the ground. Morgan pushed his face down in the dirt, hit him twice more with the gun.

He shouldered the door closed, the interior light winking out, rolled the man onto his back. A teenager, eyes half closed, nose flat and broken. Morgan could see the glint of tiny diamonds woven into his dreads.

There was an automatic in the boy's waistband. Morgan took it out, tossed it into the brush, used the bandana to wipe blood from the Beretta. Then he pushed the gun into his belt, caught the boy's wrists. He dragged him off the road and into the trees, left him facedown.

He waited, listened, then went back to the Lexus, opened the door again. When the light blinked on, he saw the AK47 propped against the passenger seat; dark wood stock, banana clip. He took it out, looked it over, pulled back the bolt to chamber a round. The selector switch was set to semi-automatic fire.

He touched the car hood. Even through the glove he could feel the engine warmth. It hadn't been here long.

He started back up the road.

Billy peered out the front window. Without a word, he leaned down, picked up the rifle, blew out the candle.

"What is it?" Sara said.

"Heard something, maybe. Keep quiet now."

A cloud crossed the moon, and the room dropped into darkness.

Morgan waited for a cloud to pass, then pushed through the trees again, the moon lighting his way. Branches slapped at him. The AK seemed to grow heavier, and twice he considered leaving it behind, but he didn't know how many of them there would be, didn't want to lose the advantage it might give him.

He was sweating freely now. Mosquitoes whined around his head. His foot caught a root and he fell hard to his knees, held on to the AK. He stayed like that, knees in the dirt, listening. He counted a long sixty, got to his feet again.

The refinery loomed closer. He kept it as his landmark, stopping every few feet to listen. When he came out onto the service road, there were shacks to his left and, parked in front of them, the dark shape of a vehicle, no one in it.

He crossed the road, followed a chain-link fence to the rear of the refinery. Through the trees, he could see the glow of light inside the building.

He found a spot where the fence sagged low, put a foot on it to push it down farther. He waited, listening. Then he stepped on the chain-link with both feet, rode it to the ground on the other side, stepped off. The sprung fence rose up wearily behind him.

Sara looked at the open door, the catwalk beyond. She could see the flickering glow of the Coleman lamp below.

Her head ached where it had hit the floor, but her vision had cleared. Billy was ignoring her, looking out into the night, the Bushmaster's forend stock resting on the sill.

She looked at the pipe again. It was maybe

three inches in diameter, with a bolted elbow sleeve holding the horizontal and vertical ends together. It would have to be old, worn. If she could work at the sleeve, she might be able to pull one of the pipes loose. Less than an inch and she could slip the cuff through.

*Then what?*

She looked at his back. If she could get free, through that door and down those stairs fast enough, she could find a way out. Would he shoot her in the back?

*If you're quick enough, he won't get the chance.*

At the window, Billy braced the butt of the rifle against his shoulder. He pointed the muzzle out into the darkness, slipped his finger over the trigger.

When he reached the edge of the trees, Morgan saw them, moving shadows against a deeper blackness. Four men. They came together in the moonlight, gathering around one of them who gave instructions with hand gestures. They all wore ski masks. The leader and another man carried rifles, the familiar silhouette of the AK. Above them, Morgan could see light in the rear windows. *That's where the money is,* he thought. *My money.*

They split up. The leader and another went around to the front of the building, one on each side. Morgan could see a rear door now. The two that were left approached it, one with an AK at port arms, the other with an automatic in a two-handed grip. They stopped a few feet from the door, as if awaiting a signal.

Morgan watched them. Years since he'd fired an AK. He lifted it to his shoulder, left hand bracing the stock, right hand closing around the pistol grip, finger sliding over the trigger. The two were about a hundred feet away, their backs to him.

He stepped out of the trees.

# TWENTY-NINE

Sara jumped when she heard the shooting. It came from behind the refinery, the flat *crack, crack, crack* of an automatic rifle.

Billy looked at her. Then they heard movement out front, and he was back at the window, firing, the AR-15 bucking, brass clattering on the concrete floor. She could hear yelling, the noise of the rifle drowning it out, echoing through the room.

He wheeled away from the window, and shots came through the empty frame, punched into the ceiling. A stray bullet sparked the wall near her, whined away inches from her ear, hit something farther back in the room. Then more shots, shouting from outside.

He took aim again, fired until the bolt locked back, swung away.

"Got the bastard that time."

He ejected the magazine, reversed it, slapped the full one in, turned back to the window.

She pulled hard on the cuff, heard the pipes rattle, pulled again, felt a little give. Then the shots and shouting were closer, and she knew they were inside.

Morgan watched the two men go down. The butt of the AK kicked against him, the barrel rising. He heard shells hit wood, break glass.

The one with the handgun rolled, got to his feet, sprinted for the left side of the building and cover. Morgan shifted his aim, squeezed the trigger, muzzle flashes making spots dance in front of his eyes. He saw splinters fly from the side of the building, heard ricochets whine off, and then the man was gone, out of sight and range.

Morgan turned, fired again at the man on the ground, bullets kicking up dirt. Then the gun was empty and smoking, the noise still echoing in his ears. He dropped it in the dirt and drew the Beretta.

Billy turned from the window, looked at her, then at the door, the catwalk. More shouting came from inside. He took the Glock, pushed it into the belt at the small of his back. The Python went into the front, butt angled to the right. He gripped the rifle.

"Billy, don't go out there. Don't do it."

Then he was through the door and gone.

When Morgan got to the man on the ground, he was facedown, motionless. Morgan kicked the AK away, went past him to the door, pulled on the handle. It rattled but didn't open.

Shots from inside, the chatter of an AK and then another gun, spaced shots. Flashes in the windows above him. He went to the loading dock, pulled himself up onto it. There was another door here, set in the wall beside the roll-up gate. He tried it. Locked. He aimed the Beretta at the keyhole, fired three times, metal fragments and wood splinters flying back at him, then kicked at the door, felt it give.

Alone in the room, Sara swiveled to look at the pipe. She pulled on the cuff again, saw her wrist was bleeding, but there was more give, the elbow sleeve looser than before.

From down below, the sound of Billy's rifle, then other shots, bullets whining off the catwalk. One flew into the room, winged off the ceiling above her. Dust drifted down.

She slid the cuff up onto the horizontal pipe, braced her hips and back against the concrete floor for leverage, raised her right foot. Outside, the popping of the Bushmaster echoed away, fell silent. Then other, scattered shots. Pistol fire.

She kicked, the heel of her sneaker thudding into the underside of the horizontal pipe. Once, twice. Pain in her heel, her ankle, but the slight squeal of metal giving way. She kicked out again, felt the pipe loosen, the sleeve almost free.

When Morgan came through the door, it was all over. Flynn stood in the center of the big room, lit by the glow of a camping lamp atop a crate. An automatic rifle lay at his feet, casings scattered on the floor. In his right hand, he held the big revolver Morgan had seen before, a Colt Python. His left was pressed against his stomach, and Morgan could see blood there. The room reeked of gunpowder.

Morgan stayed in the shadows, unseen. There were two bodies on the floor, about ten feet apart. One was facedown, an AK just out of reach. The leader. The other was slumped in a sitting position against a wall, ski mask shredded, half his head shot away, a handgun in his lap. Moths flitted around the lamp.

The leader shuddered, coughed. Flynn walked stiffly toward him.

There were three short steps from the loading dock to the main floor. Morgan went down them without a sound.

The man on the floor moaned. Flynn stood over him.

"What was that?" Flynn asked, his words slurry. "I can't hear you."

Another moan. Flynn bent, caught a fistful of the man's shirt, dragged him over onto his back. The man cried out in pain. Flynn pulled the ski mask away.

"Still can't hear you," he said and pointed the Colt at the man's face, the muzzle inches from his right eye. The man looked up at him.

*"Kolan guete . . ."* he said. *"Maman ou . . . Bouzin."* He spit.

"Didn't work out the way you planned, did it?" Flynn said and pulled the trigger.

When she heard the gunshot, Sara drove her heel up again into the pipe and it bent abruptly, the metal sleeve popping off, clattering on the floor. The two pipes sagged, ends falling away from each other. She ran the cuff along the top pipe and then it was off and she was free. She rolled to her feet.

Morgan stepped out of the shadows, pointed the Beretta at Flynn's back.

"Don't turn around," he said. "Just drop the gun."

Flynn didn't move.

"Drop it or you're dead right here, right now."

Flynn tried to straighten, the gun hung at his side.

"You can still walk away from this," Morgan said. "You just need to tell me where that money's at. But first you need to drop that gun."

Flynn gave a flat laugh that turned into a wet cough. He spit blood on the floor. Then he started to turn.

Sara looked around. No weapons in the room. She could hear talking below, then Billy's laugh, a cough. She looked at the half-open gearbag, caught it by its straps, felt its weight. Then she was out on the catwalk, looking over the railing at the two of them below, lit by the single lamp, the black man called Morgan, gun up and steady. Billy, bloody and bent, turning to face him.

Morgan's finger was tightening on the trigger when he heard the shout. He looked up and there was the woman deputy, at the catwalk railing, lifting something over her head, throwing it at him. He raised the Beretta.

She swung the bag, aiming it as best she could, the weight tearing it from her fingers. It turned over twice in its flight and Morgan stepped back, away from it, gun up, and Sara heard the shot, saw the bag jink in midair as the bullet hit it, and then it was falling the rest of the way, and she knew her only chance was gone.

Morgan stepped away and the bag thudded onto the floor with an upkick of dust, packets of money flying out. Flynn stumbled back, a hand raised against the dust. Then he saw the money, realized what it was. He brought the Python up and the woman screamed *no no no no no* and then the Python's hammer fell with a dry click on a spent shell.

Morgan shot him three times.

# Thirty

The shots sounded almost as one. Sara saw Billy spin away, the Colt fly from his hand. He twisted, fell hard, and then she was running down the stairs, and when she reached the bottom, Morgan was pointing his gun at her.

"Just stay right there," he said. "No need to come any closer."

She didn't move. After a moment, he lowered the gun, crouched, turned the bag right side up, gathered the bricks of money from the floor, put them back in, watching her. When he had them all, he tugged at the zipper, got it halfway closed. Then he lifted the bag by a carry strap, looked at her, slung it over his left shoulder. He shook his head.

"Foolish," he said. Then he turned his back on her and walked away.

Morgan went back the way he'd come. Up the steps to the loading dock, through the ruined door. The bag was heavier than he expected, the strap cutting into his shoulder. It felt good.

He scrambled down from the loading dock. The man in the dirt hadn't moved. Morgan headed for the trees.

Billy was still breathing. She ripped his shirt open, the flannel already soaked through with blood. Four entry wounds, three in the chest, one in the stomach.

He coughed once, looked up at her. *Don't die, you son of a bitch. Don't die on me. Not like this.*

"Your cell, Billy. Where is it?"

His eyes seemed to drift in and out of focus. He raised his right hand toward her.

"Where's your phone?"

She patted his jeans, felt the bulk in his right pocket. She reached in, got the phone out. A handcuff key tumbled after it.

She opened the phone, fingers slick with blood, turned it on. She waited for it to glow into life, then punched in 911. As the call went through, he touched her face gently. She could feel the warmth of his blood.

Halfway through the woods, he ejected the clip from the Beretta, replaced it with a full one. The moon was high and bright, made it easier to find his way.

He began to feel flush, hot. He stopped for a moment, let the dizziness pass, felt the first glow of pain in his right side. He caught a tree limb, held on to it for balance. The strap slid from shoulder to elbow.

He stayed that way for a moment, breathing in, filling his lungs. Then he let go of the branch, pushed the strap back up his shoulder, kept going.

She worked the key in the lock and the cuff came loose, the shiny metal smeared with her blood. She tossed the cuffs away, saw the cuts left on her wrist.

Billy's eyes were open, his chest rising and falling slowly. She'd taken the lamp from the crate, set it beside him.

"It'll be okay," she said. "An ambulance is coming. It's on its way. You're going to be all right."

He half-smiled at her and then coughed, pearls of blood on his lips. She put a palm on his face, and he laid a bloody hand over it, held it.

"It's going to be okay," she said and felt the wetness in her eyes spill onto her cheeks.

She watched the light go out of his eyes, a soft breath escape his lips. His eyes half closed, as if he'd grown drowsy without warning. His hand slipped from hers. She knew he was gone.

Morgan reached the first service road sooner than he expected. The vehicle was still there, in front of the shacks, and he saw now it was the woman's Blazer. He thought about shooting out a tire, but there was no time to waste. Others would be here soon. He had what he'd come for.

The pain was still sharp in his stomach, but the dizziness seemed to be gone. His skin felt cool where the sweat had dried.

He pushed through trees, undergrowth, branches snagging at the bag. Twice he had to stop to pull it loose. Then the trees thinned, moonlight shining through, and he was at the second road. He started down it, saw the outline of the Lexus. The driver's side door was open, the interior light on. He saw the dreadlocked boy sprawled there, half in the car, half on the road, trying to pull himself up onto the seat, his face dark with blood. Morgan raised the Beretta.

Sara could hear sirens far away. She knelt on the concrete beside him, his face turned to the side, his chest still. She'd checked his carotid pulse twice, known what she would find.

She stood, wiped her bloody hands on her jeans. The sirens grew louder.

*He's still out there, somewhere close. Maybe waiting to open fire on them when they get here. They could be driving right into it, not knowing.*

She could stay here, let him get away. Let the danger pass. No one would blame her.

She knelt again, reached beneath Billy, felt his warmth, gently tugged the Glock from his belt.

She fumbled with bolts at the front door, pushed against rusty hinges to get it open. She went out into moonlight, a wide clearing. A figure in a ski mask lay sprawled in the dirt, face up, not moving. She pointed the Glock at him as she went past.

At the metal frame gate, she bent, squeezed through the horizontal bars. Then she was on the service road, moving up it with the Glock in a two-handed grip in front of her. She saw the Blazer ahead, went around it to make sure no one was there. She looked at the dirt and saw no tire tracks other than her own.

*He didn't walk here. He's got a vehicle someplace.*

Her tac bag was in the backseat where she'd left it. She got the Kevlar vest out, pulled it on over her sweatshirt, worked the

Velcro snaps.

Then, in the distance, she heard the single gunshot.

# THIRTY-ONE

Morgan stepped over the body, started down the road to the Monte Carlo. He could hear far-off sirens.

When he reached the car, he decocked the Beretta, pushed it into his belt, got the keys out, dropped them. He felt fresh sweat on his forehead, a growing pain in his stomach. He bent, picked up the keys, and the vertigo hit him. He fell against the side of the car, put a hand on the fender to steady himself.

*Not now,* he thought. *You need to keep moving. You need to get out of here.*

He got the driver's side door open, set the gearbag on the seat, pushed it over as he got behind the wheel. He fumbled with the keys, his fingers unresponsive, dropped them again. He got the ignition key in, pulled the door shut. He ground the starter on the first try, got it going on the second.

The road was too narrow to turn around, and he couldn't risk backing up all the way down to the highway. He set the Beretta on the seat, pulled ahead. There was a clearing past the Lexus, enough room to make a three-point turn, face back the other way.

Hc swung left, cleared the car and the body, trees scratching the driver's side. He turned the Monte Carlo across the road, reversed until his rear bumper crunched into undergrowth. He had to do it twice more to bring the car's nose around.

Lights off, he looked past the Lexus, down the length of the moonlit road to the highway beyond.

Sara gunned it, driving with the windows down, listening over the sound of the engine, the growing sirens. The Glock was on the seat beside her. In the rearview, she could see two bloody fingerprints on her cheek.

Then she saw the second service road ahead, started to brake. That was where the shot would have come from, where the vehicle would be. The only place.

She barely made the turn, tires squealing, kicking up dust as she took the hard right. The Blazer clattered over the canal bridge, and the Glock flew from the seat onto the floor. She hit the gas, switched on her high beams, roared up the narrow service road.

Then she saw the car.

Morgan looked at the onrushing headlights, hit the brakes hard. The Monte Carlo's nose dipped, and the gearbag rolled off the seat and thumped on the floor.

He slammed the shifter into reverse, hit the gas, backed up toward the Lexus. The headlights came toward him. He thought about abandoning the car, heading out on foot. He wouldn't get far carrying the bag, though, and he'd come too far, done too much, to leave it.

He braked, the car rocking, shoved it into park, gripped the Beretta, and opened the door.

She saw the face through the windshield, knew it was him. She slowed, but he was reversing now, back up the road. She followed him, and then he braked hard and she had to do the same. The Blazer came to a stop about ten feet away, their grilles pointing at each other, dust swirling in her headlights.

She moved without thinking, got the Glock from the floor, pushed the driver's side door open, saw Morgan getting out, ready to run. But then he was leaning across the roof, aiming a gun at her, using the car for cover, and she crouched behind the door, the Glock in a two-handed grip over the top of it.

"Police! Don't move!"

He looked at her. The sirens were louder, closer.

*You could shoot him now. He has a weapon. He killed Billy. Do it.*

Her finger tightened on the trigger but didn't squeeze. He watched her, his gun not moving.

"Drop the weapon," she said. "Now."

When he spoke, his voice was calm. "You need to get out from there," he said, "and get out of my way."

She realized then why he'd backed up. The Blazer would have blocked the narrow road, but as he'd reversed she'd followed him into a wider clearing. There was room to get around her now, past her. If she'd stopped farther down the road, he'd have been trapped.

*Too late now.*

"Put that weapon down," she said.

"I don't want to shoot you, woman. If I did, I would have done it back there. Or let those other boys get you. But I let you be."

She was breathing shallowly, starting to hyperventilate. She tried to control it, steadied the Glock. She looked back toward the refinery, saw flashing emergency lights turning down the service road there.

"Just you and me," he said. "Nobody's going to save you. And nobody has to get hurt. Just get out of my way."

"I can't do that."

She felt sweat in her eyes, blinked it away. The Glock began to waver.

"You owe me, woman."

She was trembling, her arms spasming as if she were holding a heavy weight. The barrel clinked on the lip of the door, then again.

"Are you wearing a vest?" he said.

She steadied the gun.

"Yes," he said. "I guess you are."

Then, as if in a movie, she saw his gun angle down, the bloom of the muzzle flash. She was already squeezing the trigger when the impact hit her. A sledgehammer to the chest, the stars and moon whirling around her, and then she was on her back, the imprint of bright flashes echoing in her eyes.

*He shot you.*

She looked up at the sky, saw a shadow cross the moon. She heard a car door shut, somewhere far away, the squeal of tires. The smell of exhaust as the car passed by her, a foot from her face. She couldn't breathe, couldn't move. She closed her eyes.

*Danny.*

■ ■ ■ ■

He swung the Monte Carlo around the Blazer, steering wide of where the woman lay. As he rumbled over the metal bridge, he felt the searing pain on his right side. The familiar place. He dropped the Beretta on the seat, wrenched the wheel to the right as he reached the highway. The tires sprayed gravel and then he was on the wide road, lights out, gas pedal to the floor.

In his rearview, he saw more emergency vehicles far behind him, watched as, one by one, they turned down the service road to the refinery, their lights blotted out by the trees.

The Monte Carlo leaped ahead, the V8 growling, the moon bright enough to drive by. He was alone on the road.

How much night was left? He knew he wouldn't get far in daylight. He needed to find another car, switch plates, get out onto the interstate, head north, out of this county, out of this state.

He looked over at the gearbag, saw bits of safety glass on the seat. For the first time he saw the starred hole in the windshield, just above the dashboard.

He tugged his right glove off with his

teeth, let it fall in his lap. He pulled away the edge of the windbreaker. Just a dull ache down there, numbness, but everything was wet, warm, and he could feel it spreading down his leg. He touched his pullover on the right side, felt where the bullet had gone in.

Up ahead, a tan Florida Highway Patrol car came over a rise, siren blaring, lights flashing. It blew past him. He watched it in his rearview, waited for it to swing around, come after him. It topped another rise and was gone.

After a while, he slowed to fifty. He was unsure how long he'd been driving. The highway seemed more like a country road now. Trees on one side, sugarcane on the other. Dawn was a pink bar on the horizon. A soft whistling came through the hole in the windshield. He felt sleepy, cold.

He popped the glove box open, got a cassette out. Sam Cooke. He took it out of its case, left a bloody thumbprint on it as it slid into the player. He adjusted the volume, Sam's sweet and rough voice coming strong through the speakers. *"I was born by the river . . ."*

Tired as he was, it made him smile.

Sara rolled onto her knees, put one palm

against the ground to steady herself. The pain was a solid block across her chest.

There was a single dime-sized hole in the interior of the open door. She touched her chest, felt the indentation in the vest that matched it. She saw the Glock beneath the Blazer, out of reach.

She fell back into a sitting position then, heard something fall to the ground. She picked it up. A flattened slug.

She was still looking at it when sirens began to scream behind her. She turned, saw the first cruiser pull onto the service road, rumble over the bridge.

She put a hand on the seat for support, got her feet under her. *You can do it. You can.* The next thing she knew she was standing, wavering but standing, still holding the slug. The pain in her chest began to lessen.

She looked at the flashing lights, heard sirens, doors opening, people calling to her. Deputies with guns drawn. She saw Sheriff Hammond coming toward her. She tried to smile to show him she was all right. She couldn't.

# THIRTY-TWO

Sara stood beside an EMT van, a blanket around her shoulders, and watched them bring the bodies out. They'd tried to get her into a van, take her to the hospital — *Not yet* — and eventually Hammond had given in. Her chest hurt to the touch, but she could breathe without pain.

There were nearly a dozen emergency vehicles parked in front of the refinery, radios crackling and squawking. The sun was up, had chased the shadows away. Birds sang in the trees.

They'd dressed and wrapped her wrist, made her take the blanket because they were worried she was slipping into shock, but she knew she wasn't. One of the EMTs hovered nearby.

Elwood came up alongside her.

"Anything?" she said.

"Not yet. Statewide BOLO. Jersey plates, he won't get far."

"Sorry I couldn't get the tag number."

"Priorities, Sara. What's important is you're all right."

They brought them out on covered stretchers, one at a time, loaded them carefully into the back of the other EMT vans. When they brought the fourth stretcher out, the sheriff walked beside it, and she knew it was Billy.

She let the blanket slip from her shoulders to the ground. The sheriff came around the stretcher to head her off. The EMTs stopped where they were, unsure what to do.

She looked down at the stretcher, the rough green blanket covering him. The sheriff put a hand on her shoulder.

"Is he bagged?" she said.

"No."

She pulled the blanket down over that face. His head was tilted to the left on the stretcher, eyes half open, looking off at something only he could see.

She should feel something, she knew, but there was nothing there. Just a numbness that seemed to stretch far down into her, fill her entirely.

She reached down, and one of the EMTs said, "Hey," but the sheriff motioned to him and he was silent. She laid fingers on Billy's eyelids and gently closed them, then lifted the blanket back over his face.

She stepped away from the stretcher. The EMTs looked at the sheriff. He nodded.

They carried him away.

When he couldn't keep his eyes open any longer, Morgan found a side road that wound through the trees. The cassette had switched over to the other side. Sam still singing sweet and strong, but running out of time.

The road turned to dirt after a while, the Monte Carlo bumping back and forth. He powered the window down, could smell the woods, the cleanness of them, and something else on the breeze, a coolness.

When he came out of the trees, he was at a river. There was a clearing here, a gentle slope down to the water's edge. He pulled the Monte Carlo into the shade of a weeping willow, turned the ignition off. The engine coughed and was silent.

It's come a long way, he thought. Time to rest.

The branches of the willow moved in the breeze, brushed the top of the car. Morgan listened to the music, looked out at the river. It was moving slow, wind rippling the surface. On the far bank were more willows, another clearing, picnic tables under the trees. Early morning and no one around. The breeze that blew across the water smelled of flowers. Birds chirped in the trees.

His right shoe was full of blood, cooling now. He looked at the gearbag, wondered what was in it.

He let his head rest on the seat back, smelling the sweet air, feeling the sun on his face. And then he closed his eyes.

# THIRTY-THREE

The line rang once, twice. Sara waited, cell phone to her ear, wondered if she had the right number. The sheriff had run interference with the phone company, backtraced her home phone, gotten the number for her, hadn't asked why.

She was in the living room, lit by a single lamp. Danny was sleeping, his door half open. The house was quiet.

After the fourth ring, there was a pause and then the woman said "Who is this?"

"Sara Cross."

Silence on the line, then, "How did you get this number?"

"I just wanted to call, to tell you thanks."

Another pause. "I didn't do that for you."

"I understand."

"It was for that little boy."

"I know. That's why I wanted to thank you."

"Well, now you have. And there's no

reason to be calling this number again, is there?"

"No," Sara said. "There isn't."

"Then we're done," Simone James said, and the line went silent.

The costume wasn't quite finished. It took her three tries to get the bandana folded right. When she did, it fit neatly over his head, covering the sparseness of his hair. She tied it in back, adjusted the patch over his left eye.

"There you go, Captain."

He bounded down the hall to the bathroom, pulled up a stool so he could see himself in the mirror.

"Well?" she called to him.

"It's great!"

She went to the window, looked out. It was almost dark, the streetlights blinking on one by one. On the windowsill, beside the bowl of bite-sized candies, a candle flickered in the jack-o'-lantern she'd carved.

She heard his pounding feet, turned to see him come running back into the living room.

"Easy," she said.

"I'm ready!"

"Okay, but remember what I told you."

She straightened the big belt, the plastic

sword that hung from it.

"You going to be okay walking in those boots?"

"Sure."

"You're going to stay with me now, right? Not run ahead?"

He nodded.

She got a jacket from the closet, pulled it on. He was already waiting at the door, carrying a plastic bag that said PIRATE'S BOOTY.

He turned to look at her, and she stopped. And in that moment, she felt the fear, the uncertainty, the pain empty out of her, like something untangling inside.

"Mom, are you all right?"

She blinked at the wetness, zipped up the jacket.

"Yeah, little guy," she said. "I'm all right."

Then she took his hand, and together they walked out into the night.

The employees of Thorndike Press hope you have enjoyed this Large Print book. All our Thorndike, Wheeler, and Kennebec Large Print titles are designed for easy reading, and all our books are made to last. Other Thorndike Press Large Print books are available at your library, through selected bookstores, or directly from us.

For information about titles, please call:
   (800) 223-1244

or visit our Web site at:
   http://gale.cengage.com/thorndike

To share your comments, please write:
   Publisher
   Thorndike Press
   295 Kennedy Memorial Drive
   Waterville, ME 04901